INVASION!

Crow hunkered down in the shelter of a flight of concrete steps. Laser flashes of rifle fire came from the upper windows across the avenue, and more flashes answered them from the windows above his head.

A squad of Capellan Confederation soldiers crouched in a public transit stop, firing at the windows on the far side of the avenue. One of the CapCons threw a smoke grenade and in the next instant the air roiled with throat-clenching white fog. The CapCons shouted and rushed into the street, shadowy figures moving through the smoke. More laser fire flashed down; some of the figures fell, but others kept running. Smoke scattered the laser fire, making a light too brilliant to look at.

Then he heard the rumble of engines and the sound of metal thudding on concrete in regular, titanic footfalls. He looked to his left. Down at the end of the avenue, a looming anthropomorphic shape strode around the corner of the building, one massive arm punching out and into the third-floor windows as it came: a *Thunderbolt* BattleMech, swinging into action.

A SILENCE IN THE HEAVENS

A BATTLETECH® NOVEL

Martin Delrio

A ROC BOOK

ROC
Published by New American Library, a division of
Penguin Group (USA) Inc., 375 Hudson Street,
New York, New York 10014, U.S.A.
Penguin Books Ltd, 80 Strand,
London WC2R 0RL, England
Penguin Books Australia Ltd, 250 Camberwell Road,
Camberwell, Victoria 3124, Australia
Penguin Books Canada Ltd, 10 Alcorn Avenue,
Toronto, Ontario, Canada M4V 3B2
Penguin Books (N.Z.) Ltd, Cnr Rosedale and Airborne Roads,
Albany, Auckland 1310, New Zealand

Penguin Books Ltd, Registered Offices:
80 Strand, London WC2R 0RL, England

First published by Roc, an imprint of New American Library,
a division of Penguin Group (USA) Inc.

First Printing, June 2003
10 9 8 7 6 5 4 3 2 1

Cover design by Ray Lundgren

Printed in the United States of America

PUBLISHER'S NOTE
This is a work of fiction. Names, characters, places, and incidents either are the products of the author's imagination or are used fictitiously, and any resemblance to actual persons, living or dead, business establishments, events, or locales is entirely coincidental.

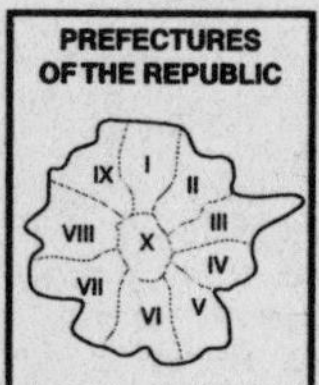

REPUBLIC OF THE SPHERE

PREFECTURES I, III, IV AND V

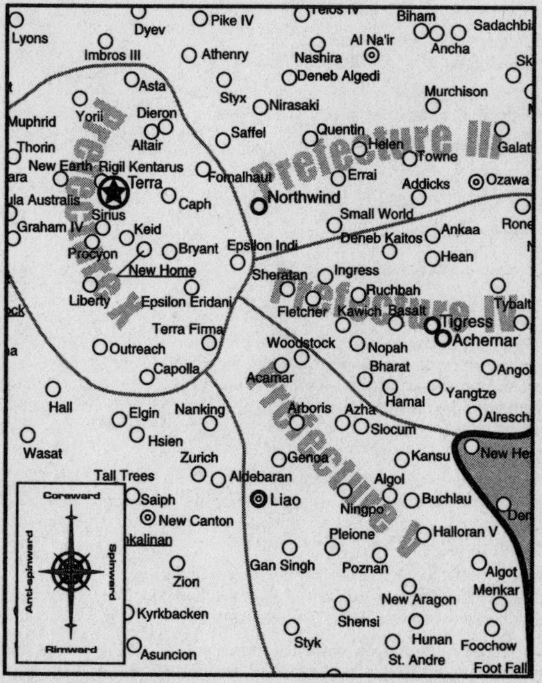

Lyons
Dyev
Pike IV
Telos IV
Biham
Sadachbia
Imbros III
Athenry
Nashira
Al Na'ir
Ancha
Asta
Deneb Algedi
Murchison
Styx
Nirasaki
Yorii
Dieron
Muphrid
Altair
Saffel
Quentin
Helen
Galatia
Thorin
Towne
New Earth
Rigil Kentarus
Fomalhaut
Errai
Addicks
Ozawa
Terra
Northwind
Caph
Sirius
Small World
Graham IV
Keid
Deneb Kaitos
Ankaa
Procyon
Bryant
Epsilon Indi
Hean
New Home
Sheratan
Ingress
Liberty
Epsilon Eridani
Ruchbah
Tybalt
Fletcher
Kawich
Basalt
Tigress
Terra Firma
Achernar
Woodstock
Nopah
Outreach
Bharat
Capolla
Acamar
Hamal
Yangtze
Hall
Arboris
Azha
Elgin
Nanking
Slocum
Alrescha
Hsien
Wasat
Zurich
Genoa
Kansu
New Hessen
Tall Trees
Aldebaran
Algol
Saiph
Liao
Buchlau
Ningpo
New Canton
Halloran V
Pleione
Gan Singh
Poznan
Algot
Zion
Menkar
New Aragon
Kyrkbacken
Shensi
Hunan
Foochow
Styk
Asuncion
St. Andre
Foot Fall
Prefecture III
Prefecture IV
Prefecture V
Prefecture X
Coreward
Spinward
Rimward
Anti-spinward

Maximum Jump approx 30 LY. For nav purposes use 9 PARSECS (29.34 LY)

8 PARSECS

40 PARSECS OR 130.4 LIGHT YEARS

PART ONE

Northwind, Winter 3132–3133
Rumors of War

1

The Fort
City of Tara, Northwind
Prefecture III, Republic of the Sphere
November, 3132; local winter

Tara Campbell, Countess of Northwind and Prefect of Prefecture III, stood alone in the Hall of Warriors in the Fort of the Northwind Highlanders. The day's meeting was done, and the chamber was empty. No grave and serious warriors watched her from their places on benches of timeworn, polished oak, looking out across data terminals and communications arrays whose bright screens and metallic reflections gave an incongruous touch of workaday modernity to the stark and ancient chamber.

The room's only illumination came from units built into the walls and ceiling—at this time of day, with the chamber mostly deserted, they put forth only a dim and murky light. Outside the

Hall of Warriors, Tara knew that the vast stone bulk of the Fort would still be touched and warmed by the last rays of the sun as it set behind the Rockspire Mountains, painting the sky above Northwind's capital city with vivid streaks of red and orange.

Away to the northern part of the Fort complex lay the New Barracks—a commonplace term for the collection of sprawling stone buildings that had housed the main elements of the Northwind Highlanders ever since they had ceased to be a far-flung mercenary force and had come home to defend their own planet instead. The main armory and the training simulators were also located in the New Barracks, as were a set of living quarters provided as a matter of regimental courtesy to the Prefect whenever he or she was resident on Northwind. Only a few months ago, those quarters would have been offered to Katana Tormark, but Duchess Tormark had broken her oath to The Republic of the Sphere, and had openly declared for House Kurita and the Dragon's Fury.

And to think I led the cheering when they first made that woman Prefect, Tara thought bitterly. I lacked the experience and the seasoning for the job, I said when my name was mentioned, and I told them to choose Katana Tormark instead. She had everything that was needed—the Academy training, the administrative experience, the impressive battlefield record—everything, it turned out, except loyalty. Now she's gone and I'm standing here in her place, and everything I said about myself, that compared to Duchess Tormark I was young and untested and green, is as true now as it was before.

But I, at least, am loyal.

She turned away from the speaker's platform and walked across the floor to the shallow stone steps that led upward to the double doors at the far end of the empty hall. The corridor outside the Hall of Warriors was likewise empty, though of more modern construction and considerably better lit.

"Working late, ma'am?"

The voice of the security guard stationed outside the chamber startled her. I'm getting jumpy, she thought.

"Yes," she said. "I was. But I'm done for the night."

"Will you be wanting an escort to your quarters?"

"Thanks, no," she replied. The walk to the Barracks wasn't long, and passed through the heart of the Fort complex. "See that all stays secure."

"Aye. Good night, ma'am."

Tara was aware of the echoes of her own footsteps as she walked down the corridor toward the elevator on the north rotunda.

The rotunda was dark, and the elevator was a glass-enclosed booth that scooted down the wall into the lower lobby. Tara found this out of place and disturbing for some reason—her mind kept telling her that this elevator belonged in the Senate Chambers on Terra, rather than here on Northwind. She told her mind to be quiet, and entered the elevator.

The door shut behind her. The elevator began to descend.

The lights everywhere were dim. Outside the walls it would be full night by now, and the entire building was deserted. That too, she thought, was wrong. The Fort was never completely empty. It was above all else a military installation, with troopers standing guard and officers on watch night and day.

She told her mind to stop picking at insignificant details, and rode the elevator down.

As she descended into the dark, a shadow moved below her—a shadow in human form. Tara looked again.

The person down there is a woman, she thought. And she moves—she moves like—

The elevator reached the bottom of its transit just as the shadow-woman moved forward. Tara gasped, but managed to maintain her composure.

"Katana!" she said.

"Yes," the other woman said. "I've come back. I've come back for you."

"I knew that you were loyal," Tara said. "But why didn't you tell me?"

"Because"—two swords whispered from their sheaths—"facing you in a 'Mech wouldn't be nearly as satisfying as slicing you to pieces hand to hand."

Tara fell backward, avoiding the twin blows that sliced through the air where she had been standing, rolled to her feet, and feinted right. A katana—the long sword of the samurai—was nothing to take on barehanded. But she didn't have a choice; the lobby of the Senate Chamber wasn't the sort of area that was full of the makings of improvised weapons.

"This is going to be fun," Katana said.

Her right-hand blade made a whistling sound as she spun it forward and down toward where Tara had moved. The second blade came in from the side, waist-high.

Tara retreated again, spinning to let the whirling steel miss her.

"Katana!" she said. "What are you doing here? And why—"

She leapt again. The last attack had come too close, slicing the cloth above her chest.

"You lured me here."

"No, it was me."

The voice came from behind them. A man's voice. The security guard. How did *he* get here? Tara wondered, in the instant before Katana brought both her blades across the space Tara had been occupying. But instead of feeling steel bite through flesh, the Duchess found herself facing a guard with a drawn handgun.

"What have you done with Tara Campbell?" he asked.

The light was dim, and getting dimmer. And Tara was . . .

. . . awake, and tangled in the sheets of her bed in the Barracks, with the early-morning sunlight hitting her in the face. She lay still for a few minutes, waiting for the adrenaline rush from the nightmare to subside. Finally, she gave up on trying to relax and rose to a sitting position.

"Never mind trying to catch a few more minutes of sleep," she said aloud. "I'm going to go over to the armory, and I'm going to fight something in a simulator that knows it's a simulator, and that I know is a simulator, and I'm going to fight it until it's dead."

She got out of bed and dressed hastily in a plain set of uniform fatigues. After a brief moment's consideration, she pulled a dark fleece changing robe out of her closet and added it to the zippered bag that held her MechWarrior's neurohelmet and cooling vest. Fighting in a simulator was almost as hot and sticky a job as fighting in a real 'Mech—the training wouldn't be any good if that weren't the case—and she didn't want to risk taking a chill when she left the simulator for the colder air outside.

The main floor of the armory was all but deserted when she entered. She exchanged salutes with the sergeant on duty at the front desk, said, "If anybody needs me in the next hour or so, I'm going to be training in the 'Mech simulator," and within minutes was exorcising the last vestiges of her nightmare in a scenario featuring a single *Hatchetman* 'Mech against two tanks, a hovercraft, and a full platoon of armored infantry.

She reduced both tanks and the hovercraft to smoking rubble within the first fifteen minutes, but the infantry proved more recalcitrant, harassing her 'Mech with rifle fire and grenades in an attempt to distract her from a fire team with a laser cannon that was maneuvering for position. The simulated game of high-firepower tag that resulted went on for almost half an hour, and had not yet reached a conclusion when the communications rig inside the simulator buzzed and crackled.

". . . Colonel Michael Griffin. . . ." it said, between bursts of static.

The outside sound pickup wasn't as good as it would have been in a real 'Mech; the audio portion in a simulation came over the internal system, and the simulator's designers had paid more attention to blocking out external noise than they did to admitting it.

". . . important news."

2

Red Ledge Pass
Bloodstone Range of the Rockspire Mountains
Northwind
November, 3132; local winter

Will Elliot whistled under his breath as he made his way down the snow-covered Red Ledge Pass. The party of well-heeled bankers and industrialists he'd been nursemaiding through the backcountry for the past two weeks had climbed aboard their chartered VTOL craft and headed home to their offices and factories on Northwind's equatorial continent. He was free and on his own, at least until he reached the trailhead and the offices of Rockhawk Wilderness Tours.

The tourists had offered him a ride in the VTOL, but that would have meant flying with them into Tara and taking ground transportation back out again. Add in all the time he'd have needed to spend waiting for connections, and hiking was actually faster, even on snowshoes in midwinter.

Besides, Will Elliot liked mountains, whatever the season, and he didn't like cities. Today was a fine bright day, the sky a pure blue so intense it almost hurt the eyes, and the snow beneath it a glittering, purple-shadowed white. The air was cold and resin-scented, and Will thought that if it had been any cleaner it would have squeaked when he breathed it.

The trail emerged from the trees and looped around a jumble of boulders mottled with the dark red and green of the hematite and magnetite ores that gave the Bloodstone Range its name. From this point Will had a good view of the Red Ledge road, a strip of macadam barely wide enough for two regular vehicles or one ForestryMech, winding along snakelike at the bottom of the narrow defile. The pewter blue waters of Killie Burn, too swift-moving to freeze over, ran beside the road.

His view didn't last long; the trail led around the rocky outcrop and back into the shelter of the forest. Will continued to follow the sometimes obscure signs and blazes for the next three hours, coming at last in late afternoon to the trailhead.

Rockhawk Wilderness Tours occupied a rustic log building near the paved lot where trail hikers parked their vehicles. Will's old Bannson-Built truck was still where he'd left it two weeks ago; he paused long enough to shuck off his backpack and heave it into the rear of the vehicle, and his snowshoes after it, before continuing across the lot to the office. He'd stop in long enough to collect his pay for the tour just completed, maybe have a cup of coffee that hadn't been boiled to death over a campfire; then he'd drive home.

The front room of the office felt hot and stuffy by comparison with the cold air of the trail. The young woman who did Rockhawk's filing and computer work looked up as he came in.

"Old Angus wants to see you," she said. She nodded her head toward the inner office. "In there."

Will stuffed his knit cap and his insulated gloves into the cargo pockets of his parka and hung it up on one of the wooden pegs that lined the office wall. "Did he say what for?"

"Not to me," she said. "Robbie was in here bitching again earlier, though."

Robbie Macallan was Rockhawk's other full-time guide. He was also the boss's son, which he fancied gave him a license to complain about minor inconveniences.

"Good thing I missed him, then," Will said, and passed on through to the inner office.

Angus Macallan had started Rockhawk Wilderness Tours in 3093 with himself as owner, office clerk, and sole employee. His first stroke of good fortune, securing work with a fishing-mad scion of House Kurita who wanted to try his luck with Northwind's mountain finnies, had been the start of an expanding network of regular offworld clients.

Advancing age had taken Angus Macallan off

the trails, forcing him to leave the heavy work to Robbie and Will, but he still had the rugged frame of the outdoorsman he had been. He was standing at the double-glazed office window, looking out at the snow beneath the trees, a tired expression on his weathered features. Robbie must really have given him an earful about something, Will thought.

"Are the boys from Halidon safely off?" Angus Macallan asked.

"Aye," Will said. "Smiling and happy, the lot of them, and wanting to come back in spring for the pebblefish."

"That's good." Angus left the window and went back over to his desk. "Sit down, Will."

Will complied. Old Angus had something on his mind, that was clear—there was nothing for it but to listen until he'd talked himself out. Just the same, Angus's next words confused him.

"You know the trouble they've been having with the HPG network."

"I've heard about it," Will said. "Mum's unhappy that she's missing the last episodes of *For Clan and Honor.*"

"Yes. Well." Angus traced a pattern with his forefinger on the wooden desktop. "If the network never comes back up . . . we have to make plans for that, you understand."

So that's what Robbie was going on about, Will thought, but didn't say it aloud. No good, after all, ever came of criticizing a man's son to his face.

"I understand," he said. "Some things will have to change."

Angus looked relieved. "I'm glad you see it that way, because without the network, we're going to lose most of our offworld bookings. Oh, a few of the regulars may still come back, but when it takes sending mail by ship to make all the arrangements, how many new clients do you think we'll be seeing?"

"There's always more clients like today's. Right here on Northwind."

"And thank God for them," Angus said. "They'll keep us from going under, if we're careful . . . but we're going to have to be very careful."

"Aye." Will kept his voice incurious and noncommittal. Whatever bad news Old Angus was working himself up to deliver, he'd get there in his own good time, and hurrying him wouldn't make it any better.

Angus sighed heavily. "We can't afford to keep on going with two guides, Will, and that's the long and the short of it. Not with the offworlders mostly gone and not coming back. I'm sorry, but that's the way it is."

"So I'm to go, and Robbie's to stay."

"It's nothing against you. It's just that with the times the way they are. . . ."

"I know." Robbie was a whinging bastard, was what he was, but he wasn't bad enough at his work that Old Angus would let him go and keep someone who wasn't family. "You'll put in a good word for me if I need one?"

"You can count on it." Angus looked a great deal happier now that he'd shifted his burden of bad news onto someone else's back.

"Thanks," Will said. He stood up. "I just need to get my money for this time, then, and I'll be gone."

"Sheila has it ready for you," Angus said. "The same as always."

"Aye," said Will, "the same as always." He went back into the outer office without bothering to close the door gently behind him. "Old Angus says you have my pay," he said to Sheila.

She pulled a long brown envelope out of the paperwork rack next to her computer and handed it to him. "It's all yours. What did the old man want?"

"To see the back of me, as it turns out," Will said. The envelope turned out to hold more than he'd anticipated; Angus had thrown in a good-performance bonus. Conscience money, Will supposed. Well, he'd take it. "There's only enough work these days for one guide, and my last name isn't Macallan."

"That isn't fair."

"Nobody's pretending it is." He put on his parka and slipped the brown envelope into an inner pocket before sealing up the front. "Take my advice and marry Robbie," he said. "That way you'll be safe if Old Angus starts worrying that there won't be enough business left to pay the office help."

3

The New Barracks
City of Tara, Northwind
November, 3132; local winter

Tara Campbell exited the 'Mech simulator as rapidly as possible, stripping out of the bulky cooling vest almost before her feet hit the floor of the armory.

She was glad she'd had the foresight to bring the plain dark changing robe with her. If the news Colonel Michael Griffin brought was important enough to drag the Prefect of Prefecture III out of a training simulation, then she didn't have time to go back to the locker room and change—and she didn't care to hold an emergency conference with the man while wearing only a snug pair of trousers and an undershirt gone nearly transparent with perspiration. Such an encounter would lack dignity, and a Prefect whom everybody—including the Prefect herself—suspected of being too young for such a high position needed all the dignity that she could scrape together.

She pulled on the robe and belted it tight around her waist, then hurried across the polished floor of the armory to meet Colonel Griffin. She would have preferred the chance to shower first, because even in a simulator a MechWarrior inevitably worked up a heavy sweat. But the officer had said that his news was urgent, and she wanted to make it clear to everyone that she took such messages seriously. Filling Duchess Katana Tormark's elegant samurai shoes was going to be hard enough without alienating the very people who were supposed to be helping her do the job.

Colonel Griffin was a lean man with close-trimmed light brown hair and a brushy but well-maintained mustache. His uniform was fresh and crisply pressed, and the medals on the breast of his tunic spoke of an eminently respectable though not flamboyant service career. In the yellow sunlight that slanted down from the windows high under the armory's vaulted ceiling, he could have passed for an artist's depiction of old style military spit and polish. Seeing him, Tara felt even more conscious than before of her own sweat-flattened hair and informal garb.

She put her chin up. She was a MechWarrior and a Campbell of Northwind, whatever she was wearing, and no mere Colonel of infantry was going to stare her out of countenance—though she suspected already that it was not

Griffin's position as a field commander that had brought him to the armory this morning, but his secondary assignment as the officer in charge of the Regiment's intelligence network here on Northwind.

"Colonel Griffin," she said, giving him her most practiced gracious smile. A precocious childhood as the diplomatic community's poster darling, she reflected, had its occasional uses even in her current position. When she absolutely had to, she could charm almost anybody. "I'm afraid the simulator isn't very good about picking up external voices—you said something about important news?"

"There's a DropShip coming into the spaceport in a few days," Colonel Griffin said. "They sent word ahead. They've got a Paladin on board, coming to help us out here on Northwind."

Tara felt her smile turn cynical, and couldn't help but feel a twinge of regret at her own reaction. There had been a time when word of a Paladin's imminent arrival would have caused her to feel a surge of anticipation that was almost hero worship, even though the newcomer's identity remained as yet unknown. But that was before Katana Tormark's betrayal had left her with the responsibility for keeping peace and good order in Prefecture III—under the current circumstances, such a gift from the Exarch, coming unasked-for as it did, was likely to prove in the end a double-edged sword.

" 'Just one Paladin?' " she said, quoting the age-old joke.

" 'Just one planet,' " Griffin said, finishing it.

She relaxed a little; the Colonel apparently shared her decidedly mixed feelings on the subject of unanticipated aid from that quarter.

"I don't suppose the Exarch and the Senate have bothered to let us know exactly what problems this Paladin is supposed to be helping us out with," she said.

If the problem that had caused Exarch Damien Redburn to send a Paladin to Northwind turned out to be only Katana Tormark's unanticipated defection to the Dragon's Fury, Tara decided that she was going to be more than a little angry. Redburn might as well have pinned a sign on the new Prefect's back saying KICK ME—I'M INEXPERIENCED! Any help a Paladin might give to Northwind in the immediate future would be paid for with years of diminished credibility for Prefect Tara Campbell afterward.

"Nothing official has come in so far," Colonel Griffin said. "I expect that the Paladin is carrying his instructions with him, and plans to brief us all upon his arrival."

"I'll just bet he does," Tara said.

She caught a strand of her hair between her fingers and twisted it thoughtfully. She'd picked up the habit as a child, when her wavy auburn locks had made her a poster photographers' darling, and the nervous gesture had survived into her angry adolescence, when she had cropped her hair rebelliously short and dyed it platinum blond. Now, in her adulthood, she still had short, spiky blond hair—and in periods of stress, she still played with it while she thought. "You said that nothing official has come in."

"That's right."

"Unofficially . . . what do our own intelligence people think is going on?"

"Based on rumors that we've heard about trouble brewing on Towne," Griffin said, "and taking into account our own recent clashes with supporters of the Dragon's Fury on Addicks, our people think the Exarch is worried that somebody is going to make a try for Terra by going through Northwind."

"Considering that those of us who actually live here have been worried about the same thing ever since this business started," Tara said, "that's no surprise."

She drew a deep breath and let it out slowly, trying to send out her irritation and paranoia along with it. Damn the fanatics, whoever they were, who had wrecked the HPG network and crippled The Republic of the Sphere; damn Katana Tormark for abandoning The Republic in favor of allegiance to a faction that Devlin Stone's years of labor were supposed to have made obsolete; and while she was at it, damn the Senate and Damien Redburn for saddling her with this ambiguous gift.

After a moment, the anger faded, and she went on. "All right. We'll assume—for public consumption, at least—that the Senate and the Exarch have recognized Northwind's special position as part of Terra's first line of defense, and that the presence of this Paladin signifies a recognition on Terra's part of Northwind's importance."

Colonel Griffin looked curious. "Do you really believe all that?"

"Not particularly," she said. "Which is why I want our people to keep working on it. If they've got any ideas about which factions constitute potential threats—other than 'every single one of them, because they've all gone crazy'—I want to have the reports waiting on my desk by the time the Paladin makes landfall."

"That shouldn't be a problem," Colonel Griffin said.

"Good." She pulled on her hair again, thinking hard. "Another thing. First impressions are important. The governor is undoubtedly going to have an official meet-and-greet for our illustrious visitor; but the Northwind Highlanders need to have their own official reception for him as well, just to make sure everybody understands that—Paladin or no Paladin—the Regiment is the host on this planet, and he's the guest."

"An excellent idea."

"I didn't spend my formative years tagging along after a couple of diplomats without learning something from the experience," she said. "For the reception, we'll need to pull together a theme that emphasizes Northwind's local traditions and autonomy on the one hand and our loyalty to The Republic of the Sphere on the other."

"I have an idea or two about that," Griffin admitted.

"Good," she said. "Then you have the whole job. I'd probably have asked for you anyway, because I want somebody from local intelligence in on the planning—you and I both know that the security aspects of this affair are going to be hellish."

4

Elliot residence
Village of Liddisdale, Northwind
November, 3132; local winter

Night had fallen by the time Will Elliot reached his mother's house in Liddisdale. Most of the shops clustered around the town's central green had already closed, except for the fuel station and the all-night pharmacy, and the streetlights had come on. He parked the BannsonBuilt in the cottage's attached garage next to his mother's electric runabout, stowed his parka and boots in the mud room between the garage and the house proper, and went inside.

The kitchen smelled of pot roast and fresh bread, and the lingering spiciness of baked fruit. His mother had made a berry tart earlier; he saw it waiting on the counter by the stove.

Jean Elliot came bustling into the kitchen and

enveloped her son in a warm hug. "It's good to see you home, Will."

"It's good to be home. You didn't have to hold up supper on my account."

"I wouldn't have cooked such a big meal if I didn't plan on sharing it with you," she said. She stepped back and gave him a gentle push. "Go clean yourself up while I get the table ready."

Half an hour later, scrubbed clean of mud and wood smoke and dressed in fresh clothes, Will joined his mother in the dining room. She'd brought out the good plates and the good table linen and her wedding silver, causing him to wonder for an instant if today was some special occasion whose significance he had forgotten. Then he remembered how, when his sisters were home, his mother had always liked to make at least one day a week a proper sit-down dinner—"for the sake of civilizing the heathen," as she had put it—and he decided that she must be feeling nostalgic.

For the first several minutes of the meal, he said nothing, only ate hungrily to make up for all the self-heating dehydrated rations he'd had to consume for breakfast, lunch, and dinner while out on the trail. Finally they reached dessert, and he was slowing down enough to say, as he took a slice of the berry tart, "I had a talk with Old Angus today."

"Ah," said his mother, looking unsurprised. "I thought you might have something on your mind."

"He's worried about the HPG network still

not coming on-line. Doesn't know how the guiding business is going to do if his offworlders can't get in touch and don't come back."

"Angus Macallan's nobody's fool. Bridie Casimir, down at the grocery, said that a DropShip came into Tara this morning with news that there's been more fighting—on Addicks, this time. People aren't going to be planning expensive vacations on foreign worlds as long as things like that are going on."

Will took a forkful of tart. The flaky crust fragmented into little pieces under the pressure, and the tines of his fork clattered against the china beneath. He looked down at his hand for a moment. A splash of purple berry juice stained the white tablecloth by his plate.

"Sorry," he said. "I'll wash it later."

His mother waved the offer away. "No matter. What did Old Angus say to you that's upset you so?"

"He's worried, like I said. Planning for the future. And he doesn't think the business is going to be able to afford two guides for much longer."

"So he's letting you go?"

"Aye."

"The stingy old bastard." Will had never heard his mother use bad language before; he was too startled by it now to say anything. "And to think I almost married him, back in '04."

He finally found his voice again. "Maybe you should have. He's kept Robbie."

"Hold your tongue. Angus Macallan could

never hold a candle to your father, God rest him." She straightened her shoulders and drew a deep breath. "Have you thought about what you're going to do next?"

Will nodded. The house itself was paid for, and a small annuity came in every month from his father's pension, but Rockhawk Wilderness Tours had made the difference between comfort and genteel poverty for both of them ever since John Elliot had died. "I have my money for the last two weeks, and a bit of a good-bye payment to sweeten it. With what we have put by, that should give us a little time."

"You're a fine outdoorsman," she said. "It won't take long to find someone else who'll take you on."

"I don't think so." Driving home in the growing dark, he'd had plenty of time to think things over and come to an unhappy conclusion. "Old Angus is one of the best, and if he's feeling the pinch then everyone else is feeling it twice as hard." He poked at the remains of his tart with his fork. "There isn't going to be any work here, not if the whole region's sliding. The best I could hope for is a job in the lumber mill down by Harlaugh, and that pays less than half what I was getting from Old Angus. I'm going to have to go away."

"I was afraid you'd want to do something like that."

"I don't want to," he said. He'd known she wouldn't be enthusiastic about losing him; both his older sisters had married and moved off some years before, one to a long-distance transport driver who worked out of Kildare on the other side of the Bloodstones, and the other to a mining engineer in Kearny. He was the only child who had remained close to home. "But if I'm going to end up looking for work in Tara anyway, I'd rather do it before every third worker in Liddisdale gets the same idea."

5

DropShip **Dark Rosaleen,** ***en route to Northwind***
Prefecture III, The Republic
November, 3132

The DropShip *Dark Rosaleen* was six days into its twelve-day journey from Northwind's Jump Point to the planet's main spaceport. Ezekiel Crow, Paladin of the Sphere, had been a silent presence among the handful of passengers, occupying his cabin—and the minds of the others aboard the DropShip—in much the same uncommunicative but hard to ignore fashion as his great *Blade* BattleMech occupied its berth in the largest of the vessel's cargo holds.

In the Paladin's case, the silence had a purpose: He had spent the first half of his journey in intensive study, ignoring the company of his fellow passengers for the company of text files and video clips. By now, Ezekiel Crow knew everything that The Republic of the Sphere's diplomatic and intelligence services had seen fit to tell him about the planet Northwind itself, and about the young and good-looking Prefect who was, arguably, its most famous living citizen.

He knew, for example, that Northwind was the second planet out from a G2I-type star, with a temperate climate—as climatologists reckoned "temperate," at any rate, which merely meant that the range of temperatures in most places didn't often go outside what a properly equipped human body could endure. Of Northwind's three continents, the greater part of New Lanark—where the capital was located—and the mineral-rich second continent of Kearny would still be in the grip of winter when he arrived. The third and smallest continent, Halidon, would be in the waning days of its summer dry season.

Crow shook his head, thinking about it. "Temperance in all things," he murmured.

But people had been freezing in the snows and parching in the deserts of temperate worlds all across the Inner Sphere for as long as humanity had been keeping track. Temperance was misleading, and Ezekiel Crow did not believe in allowing himself to be misled.

Prefect Tara Campbell, Countess of Northwind, was in many ways an even more disquieting factor than the planet of Northwind itself. The young Countess's family history and her dossier of public service were matters of common knowledge. Crow knew, therefore, of her birth off-planet to Colonel Jon Campbell and Republic Senator Moelene Jaffries-Campbell; and of her childhood stint as the darling of the news and entertainment media in the aftermath of the Capellan Campaign. He also knew of her outstanding record at the Northwind Military Academy, and of her appointment—more or less by acclamation—to the position recently vacated by Katana Tormark.

The files Crow had been given contained several likenesses of Tara Campbell, all of them recent pictures from open sources. She was a petite, platinum-haired woman who, at least in her official appearances, bore only a slight resemblance to the precocious auburn-haired moppet whose likeness had won the hearts of so many back in her poster days. What Crow wished he knew, and what he had been sent to Northwind at least partially in order to find out, was whether the Countess's delicate appearance was as misleading as the term "temperate" applied to the climate of a habitable world.

She was, undeniably, young for the position that she held. She had a rash streak in her, as well. One of the tri-vid clips had been particularly disturbing. Ezekiel Crow searched for the file amongst the others in her dossier, found it, and sent it to his cabin's display unit.

The air above the unit filled for a moment with static fog, then resolved into the image of a crowded street. A reporter armed with a microphone—and followed, Crow guessed, by a videographer—eeled his way through the press and up onto the wide marble steps of a looming piece of governmental architecture. Either by accident or by deliberate timing, the reporter reached the top of the steps just as the Countess of Northwind emerged from within the building.

The reporter stepped forward and extended the microphone, while at the same time deftly blocking Tara Campbell's further progress down the steps.

"Countess!" he said. "What's your reaction to Kal Radick's suggestion that The Republic of the Sphere should be supplanted by a new Star League?"

The reporter's videographer brought the focus zooming in tightly on Tara Campbell. In the close-up, Ezekiel Crow could see how much the question angered her: The color rose in her fair-skinned face, her blue eyes darkened, and her full lips thinned.

"The Star League's time is past," she snapped at the reporter. "Perhaps Kal Radick's time is past as well."

Watching the videographed encounter yet again, Ezekiel Crow wished that he knew for certain whether the Countess's sharp retort had been made in the heat of the moment, or if it had been an intentional provocation thrown out at the first opportunity.

Kal Radick had certainly reacted as if the insult had been deliberate. The Prefect of Prefecture IV had come within a hairsbreadth of formally demanding that Tara Campbell meet him for a Trial of Grievance.

The Countess, for her part, had either ignored or affected to ignore all of the Wolf Clansman's angry protests, and had made no direct response at all to his angry comments. Her actual reply to Radick's demand—"If he feels slighted, I invite him to Northwind where we can discuss matters in a calm and civil manner"—could have been mere empty speechmaking. On the other hand, the reply could have been exactly what it must have sounded like to Kal Radick: She was daring the Wolf to attack.

Ezekiel Crow closed down his computer files for the evening and stretched out on his bunk, dimming the lights with a gesture in the direction of the cabin's environmental sensors. He might as well start getting his body accustomed now to the length of Northwind's days and nights.

His mind, unfortunately, showed no interest in relaxing and going to sleep. Instead, he kept on thinking about the ins and outs of the situation—and the players—on Northwind.

Bad enough, Crow thought, if Tara Campbell's words had been accidental. Youth and outraged patriotism, confronted with a question posed unexpectedly, and given no chance to prepare a more considered response, could have worked together to produce a hasty reply that could be understood even if not excused. But if the provocation had been deliberate—if the young Countess had intentionally given offense to the man who was now the leader of the Steel Wolves, and had done so in a way that all but invited that faction into battle on Northwind—then the future looked bleak indeed.

It'll be Liao all over again, he thought, *if we*

can't stop it in time. Death everywhere, and blood ankle deep in the streets . . .

. . . the night sky an ugly red-brown in the lurid glow of the burning DropPort . . .

. . . a man's high-pitched screams, going on for long minutes without stopping . . .

. . . silence, worse than the screams . . .

. . . bodies scraped up like garbage and tipped by the 'Mechload into mass graves. . . .

Helpless against the onslaught of memories, he closed his eyes and let the rush of images bear him away once more into nightmare.

6

City of Chang-an, Liao
Prefecture V, Republic of the Sphere
October 3111, local summer

Twenty-two years before, the night sky over Chang-an had been a lurid red, shot through with yellow and streaked with black. The wind that blew across the city stank of smoke and spilled fuel and the sour nose-prickling smell of Gauss rifles in prolonged use. It carried with it the heavy crump of explosions, the crash of structures collapsing into rubble, the tumult of voices shouting and screaming.

He was running, dodging through the streets, trying to make it home on foot. He'd seen the Liao Conservatory of Military Arts go down, seen the main building collapse into itself when the missile hit, seen the pillar of smoke and flame rising into the sky. The deed was necessary, he knew, for those on the other side—the cadet corps had been holding the Conservatory in force with small arms and at least one autocannon. Still—minutes ago the school had been there, and now there was nothing where it had stood except craters and a pile of rubble.

He was out of breath, stumbling as he ran. He'd come on foot all the way from the DropPort. Hours and hours it had taken—walking fifty paces, running fifty, walking fifty again, as he'd been taught in his military training to reserve his strength—and he hadn't dared to grab a vehicle for any of it, because that would have made him too good a target.

The streets were blocked by people trying to escape the city, and choked with Liao defense forces coming in, while the invaders poured from the DropShip and spread out into the city like ink into water. When he'd seen on the news-screens the path the invaders were taking, and the places where resistance was gathering to meet them, he knew that he had to go home. Not to his own small bachelor apartment near the Port, but to the house he had grown up in, where his parents still lived—right along the path where the forces would collide. Were now colliding.

He saw Xin Sheng Boulevard ahead at last, a broad avenue running through the heart of the city from the business district to the Hall of Civic Governance. He had to cross it, one way or another. Home lay beyond, in a city neighborhood of town houses grouped around open squares. His parents had chosen to live in that district because of him—children could play safely in the squares, watched over by parents and nannies and the vigilant local police.

Now Xin Sheng Boulevard ran like a river of destruction in his path. He crouched in the shelter of a flight of concrete steps leading up to a first-floor office—the nameplate next to the door read HARMONIOUS VOYAGING TRAVEL AGENCY. The office's windows were all broken, and the room inside was dark. Laser flashes of rifle fire came from the upper windows across the avenue, and more flashes answered them from the windows above his head.

A squad of Capellan Confederation soldiers crouched in the shelter of a public transit stop, firing at the windows on the far side of the avenue. One of the CapCons threw a dark green smoke grenade, and in the next instant the air roiled with throat-clenching white fog. The CapCons shouted and rushed into the street, moving like shadowy figures through the smoke. More laser fire came flashing down; some of the shadowy figures fell, but the others kept on running. The smoke scattered the laser fire, making a light too brilliant to look at.

Then he heard the rumble of engines and the sound of metal thudding on concrete in regular, titanic footfalls. He looked to his left. Down at the Hall of Civic Governance end of the avenue, a looming anthropomorphic shape strode around the corner of the building, one massive arm punching out and into the third-floor windows as it came: a *Thunderbolt* BattleMech, swinging into action. He had no chance at all of crossing the avenue now.

In desperation, he backtracked a block to a transit tunnel entrance, and plunged down its steps into the dark. He paused at the bottom to let his eyes adjust—as he'd hoped, the battery-powered emergency lights were on, and the tunnel was illuminated by their crimson glow. He didn't see either CapCons or defenders anywhere nearby. If the transit cars were no longer running, he could follow the tunnel down one—no, two—stops, then go up and through the Governance Center subterranean concourse to get out, and make it home that way from the other side.

Please, he thought, let them have gotten out in time.

He lowered himself off the platform and down onto the tracks, taking care to stay away from the electrified rail in case the power should unexpectedly return. That was not the way he wanted to go out, stumbling onto his death by mistake, not with his city, with his entire planet, being murdered wholesale overhead. The air down here was hard to breathe, heavy with chemicals and foul-smelling smoke. He couldn't feel any vibration in the rails underfoot—as he'd hoped, all the trains were either stopped or dead.

He trotted down the tunnel, from one dim patch of red light to the next. A platform opened out ahead—the first stop—he kept moving, going on into the dark. At the second stop, he swung himself up onto the platform, barely noticing the pain when he banged his knee against the edge, and climbed the frozen steps of an escalator into the Governance Center concourse.

On a typical day, thousands of people passed through the concourse's vast rotunda; at any given moment, it could hold several hundred. Today, after the fighting had passed through and reduced its stores and kiosks to wreckage, it was empty—no, not quite empty. As he made his way around the perimeter of the concourse, he saw half a dozen people, office workers by their clothing, huddled together inside what had been a coffee shop. One of them at least appeared badly hurt, a business-suited woman lying half across the lap of an older, stouter, secretary-looking female. The clothes of both women were soaked with blood.

He would have gone on, intent on his self-imposed mission, if a young man in a coffee shop worker's uniform hadn't pushed himself to his feet and come forward. Here was somebody, at least, who hadn't left his post—loyalty above and beyond, wasted on "cream-no-sugar" and "double espresso" and "I'm-sorry-we're-all-out-of-that."

The coffee shop worker asked him, "Do you know if it's safe yet outside?"

He shook his head. "Not yet. There's fighting all over."

"Please," said the secretary-woman. She looked down at the woman who lay across her lap. "She's dying. Please, can you call for help, or send someone, or—"

"I can't," he said. "I don't think there's anybody left to come."

Another one of the customers spoke up—a businessman, gray-haired and well-tailored under all the dirt and blood. "Do you know if it's true what they were saying before the news channels went dark? That we were betrayed?"

He felt the bitter anger rising up in him like a poisonous spring. He had not thought he could hate so much. "Betrayed," he said. "Yes. That's the word."

Hard-eyed, the secretary-woman said, "I hope he burns."

"Yes," he said again, and felt a wave of dizziness pass over him—the lack of good air, he told himself groggily, here in the downbelow. Somebody pressed something cool into his hand; when his head cleared, he saw it was the young man in the coffee shop uniform with a chilled bottle of spring water.

"Here. Drink some, pour the rest over your head—we've got plenty in the cooler and I don't think the manager is going to be in tomorrow to check the inventory."

The water was good; it soothed his throat and cooled his skin. "Thank you," he said. "I have to go now—my parents, in the Garden Square district—I have to see if they made it out."

"Good luck," said the older businessman. "Good luck," came from the others in a murmured echo.

Then he was running again, around the perimeter of the concourse to the broad marble stairs going up into the light above. He slowed as he neared the street level, taking time to look and listen.

The street was empty, and the sounds of fighting were distant; the invaders had moved on. They had left behind the marks of their passage: overturned and burned-out vehicles; the marks of missile impacts in the cratered road; gaping holes in roofs and walls; trees and bushes shredded into mulch. A man—not CapCon, or local defense, but a civilian—lay dead near the transit entrance, crumpled and bloody in a limbs-not-meant-to-go-that-way heap.

He was running hard now. Two blocks, five blocks. In Allard Square, he saw the turf chewed and shredded by vehicles, and the children's swings and climbing tower knocked into a pile of timber and twisted metal. Six more blocks, and he came to the row of gray stone town houses each with their marble steps and downstairs bay window and tiny front garden with flowers and trees in wooden tubs.

There was the house with the green door and the bronze dragonhead door knocker. He ran up the steps. The door wasn't locked; it wasn't even latched. It swung open when he touched—when he half-fell—against it. He stumbled into the front hallway.

The cherry-wood table with the big bronze bowl on it—it had stood there all during his childhood; he used to lean his forehead against the bowl's cool metal on hot summer days—was knocked over now, the bowl rolled away into a corner and the flowers it had held scattered across the entry hall in a diagonal stripe, and spilled water everywhere.

He saw muddy boot prints on the stairway carpet, going up.

And everything else was silence.

7

The New Barracks
City of Tara, Northwind
November, 3132; local winter

The day after she received word of the Paladin's imminent arrival, Tara Campbell met with Colonel Michael Griffin in her New Barracks office. The room was small and plainly furnished—all of its contents were standard Regimental issue, and could have occupied an office on any world where the Highlanders had a fighting presence—but it was her personal sanctum, and she had chosen it deliberately over any of the more formal chambers in the Fort proper.

She felt the oppressive weight of history less in these rooms than she did in the historic structures of the Fort, and found them generally more comfortable. The heat in the Barracks office could be adjusted to an individual's preference, for one thing. The Fort's environmental controls, by contrast, had a global setting, determined in the secret recesses of the maintenance department by a combination of energy efficiency and ancient custom that Tara had never been able to figure out. She inevitably found the rooms in the Fort proper either too chilly or too warm.

Today, the weather outside her office was foggy and cold; the city was not showing its best face. Tara felt sorry that she wouldn't be able to spend more of the winter at Castle Northwind, the private residence of the Count or Countess of Northwind and the location of many of her fond childhood memories. She let herself relax for a moment, remembering Castle Northwind's crackling hearths and forested grounds, and the winters when she would go sledding down the long hill above the lake and make angels in the snow.

"Did you ever make snow angels, Colonel Griffin?" she asked absently, as she pulled up the files she wanted onto her computer screen. "When you were young, that is?"

He shook his head. "I grew up on the Oilfield Coast, in Kearny. No snow—"

"That's too bad."

"—but a great deal of sand and sunshine."

He sounded as if he missed it, and she made a note of the thought. The long, gray winters in the capital affected some people adversely, and perhaps the Colonel was one of them. She'd never hear it from him, though, if that were the case. He had the look and manner of one of the old-style Regimental officers—the ones who would consider it bad form to mention that they were mortally wounded and bleeding to death in their boots. Such stoicism was useful to a commander in desperate times, when nothing could be done about the problem, but less so when it could mean losing a good officer to the slow erosion of a treatable malaise.

Right now, however, other problems demanded Tara's attention. She opened the topmost file on her computer and turned the screen around so that both she and Colonel Griffin could see it.

"I wanted to talk with you," she said, "about the Prefectural Intelligence report."

Griffin didn't glance over at the display screen, although Tara could tell—from the way she could see him actively *not* looking at it—that she'd already piqued his curiosity enough to make him want to do so.

"I'm afraid I'm not cleared at that level," he said.

She snorted. "I'm the Prefect. If I say you're cleared, you're cleared. And I want you to see this because it concerns Northwind directly."

"In what manner, ma'am?"

The Colonel still hadn't looked at the screen, but his entire bearing had changed at her words. He was now projecting firmly restrained eagerness to be about the work she was undoubtedly planning to assign to him. Tara suppressed a smile. Griffin was one of the old style, indeed.

"Prefectural Intelligence," she said, "believes that one or more of the factions that have arisen in the aftermath of the HPG net breakdown is likely to make a try for the conquest of Terra. By way of Northwind."

Colonel Griffin's expression changed again. "That's . . . not good," he said.

Tara wondered if that masterful piece of understatement meant that he was thinking the same thing that she had thought when she first read PrefIntel's report. An invasion, if it came, would mark the first time in living memory that there had been war on Northwind.

Nobody on this world was accustomed to war anymore. They didn't know what a city park smelled like after foot soldiers with Gauss rifles had been killing each other in it for seven days, or what a once-charming country villa looked like after its roof and walls had been crushed under the foot of a 'Mech. The Vale of Flowers on Sadalbari had been a lovely place until the Black Dragon pirates set up shop there and The Republic decided to root them out.

Tara herself had come out of that campaign with a brightly glowing reputation. News sources across the Sphere fell with eagerness upon the story of the "Angel of Sadalbari," the young officer who had saved the day when her Colonel was taken out of action by 'Mech failure in the midst of battle. She'd even been featured on the cover of *Republic Today*—although the article inside had made the fighting on Sadalbari, and its aftermath, sound a great deal cleaner and more romantic than she recalled.

" 'Not good' sums up my reaction as well," she told Colonel Griffin after a moment. "This report gives Prefectural Intelligence's assessment of the relative likelihood of attack by the various known factions. When you read it, you'll see they give the best odds to the Dragon's Fury, the Steel Wolves, and Duke Aaron Sandoval and his Swordsworn, in that order. I want you to read the report and give me local intelligence's opinions on the same issue."

"Yes, ma'am," he said. "If I may?"

He reached over and tapped out the command to transfer a copy of the file to his own computer.

Tara continued. "I have to tell you, Colonel, that I already agree with PrefIntel on at least one thing: This world is in grave danger. And I believe that we must take steps to protect it."

"Do you have any plans?"

"There's a lot of things that we can't do until we know for certain who the enemy will be," she said. "Other things, though . . . we can up the strength of the Regiments. I've already authorized a heavy recruitment drive; I can do that much on my own, by virtue of my position as Countess of Northwind."

Tara saw that the Colonel was nodding as she spoke. He was on her side in this, definitely. That was good. She was going to have to push the recruitment drive through the full Council, and the long years of peace had left its members less than entirely willing to increase the size and strength of the Regiments. She couldn't share the most telling details of PrefIntel's report without compromising the intelligence that it contained. Under those circumstances, a strong voice on her side would help.

"What about equipment?" Griffin asked. "Recruiting alone isn't going to be enough."

"True," she said. She called up another file. "This is our best estimation of current needs. As you can see, due to our recent deployment of forces on Addicks and elsewhere, we have a grand total of two BattleMechs currently available on-planet: my own *Hatchetman* and the *Koshi* belonging to the planetary reserves. Any invasion force we encounter is almost certain to bring more 'Mechs than that into play. Suggestions?"

"Word from our off-planet intelligence sources is that local defense forces across the Sphere have begun making effective use of converted ForestryMechs and IndustrialMechs. We have a good number of those available, as well as MiningMechs and ConstructionMechs."

"Yes," she said. "But we can't commandeer all of them. There are people relying on those 'Mechs to keep their businesses going. If we save the planet from invasion only to have the economy crash afterward, we won't have helped things very much."

"If we can't save Northwind from invasion, the state of the economy isn't going to matter," Griffin pointed out.

"It's not that simple," she said. "A victorious campaign coupled with a wrecked economy leaves us wide open for a takeover by the next faction that's willing to have a try. Our ancestors fought too long and too hard for a free world of their own—we can't betray them by throwing it away."

"We're still going to need those 'Mechs."

"Then find somebody in your department who knows economics and can do the math," she told him, "and have him or her figure out what percentage of the available 'Mechs we *can* take and retrofit for combat without damaging the planetary infrastructure beyond repair."

Finally he gave a slow nod. "I have a couple of people I could put on that job."

"Good. And get somebody else to start talking with the firms that actually produce all those working 'Mechs. Find out if they can start adding a certain number of . . . ah . . . preconfigured fighting models to each production run."

"I can do that myself," he said.

"Assign someone else to it if you can," she said. "I want you to jaunt down to the Aerospace Branch of the Academy, on Halidon—they'll need to know that there's trouble in the wind, and that they're as much a part of the defense mix as any of the units on Kearny or New Lanark."

She paused and added, smiling, "It's summer down there. Take a day or two of your accumulated leave, Colonel, and enjoy the sand and sunshine because once that Paladin gets here, I don't think any of us are going to make it out of the city for quite a while."

8

Commercial District
City of Tara, Northwind
December, 3132; local winter

Winter in the Bloodstone Range had been clean and snow-clad and cold. Winter in the capital city of Tara, Will Elliot had found, could be clammy and unpleasant. The streets were filled with dirty puddles of half-melted slush and raked by a raw, incessant wind that felt like it had come straight down from the polar regions without encountering so much as a strand of electric fencing by way of a windbreak.

The weather alone was not so bad—the mountains were much colder, and often as wet—but the air in the city smelled of garbage and chemicals and close-pressed humanity, and vibrated with the strident clamor of people and machines. Even the Great Thames River, clean and fast-running when it came out of the mountains north and west of Harlaugh, in Tara had been cramped and channeled and forced to run through concrete ditches.

He could have endured everything, he thought, if there had only been work. But so far, the time he'd spent living in a rooms-by-the-week hotel and eating generic-label microwave dinners for his one meal each day had failed to turn up any useful possibilities. He didn't have the right kind of education, or enough of the education that he did have, to apply for office work; he wasn't a member of the trade organization that controlled hiring and labor at the DropPort; and the few jobs that he could have gotten paid less than living in Tara cost, and would leave him with no time in which to search for something better.

He was on his way back to his rented room after another fruitless day of searching when he saw the poster in the shopfront window:

NORTHWIND HIGHLANDER REGIMENT:
STANDING GUARD
ASK ABOUT OUR ENLISTMENT BONUS
AND VALUABLE TRAINING OPPORTUNITIES

The poster's artwork depicted a young woman in full-dress uniform standing next to the foot of a BattleMech. On the outside wall next to the display window hung a metal rack full of brightly printed flyers, all of them bearing titles like "Regimental Advanced Education Program: Learn While You Serve" and "Earth, Space, and Sky: Aerospace Fighter Command" and "Your Pay and Benefits."

Will peered through the glass door at the room inside—a quick glance only, for the sake of appearing casual rather than increasingly desperate. He saw a man in uniform, with medals, sitting at a desk in the front of the office. A door in the wall behind the desk opened into another room, but Will couldn't make out what lay on the other side. The man in uniform was talking to a nervous-looking young woman in regular clothing; she sat in a straight chair on the other side of the desk.

The diner across the street had a cheap lunch special, a hot meat pie and choice of two vegetables. Will decided that he could afford to treat himself this once. One way or another, he wasn't going to be needing to stretch out his dwindling supply of cash much longer. So far, nothing he'd found in the capital had turned out to be better than the Harlaugh mill; he'd probably be heading back there tomorrow anyway.

He picked up a copy of the "Pay And Benefits" flyer to read while he ate. By the time he'd finished the meat pie and paid for his meal, the girl had left the recruiting office and the chair across the desk from the man in uniform was empty. Will pushed open the door and stepped inside.

He went up to the desk and said quickly, before he could change his mind, "I want to enlist."

The man in uniform—from this close, Will

could see that the name plate on his desk read Master Sergeant Dylan ap Rhys—looked him up and down and said, "If you're here because you want to be a MechWarrior, you might as well turn around now and go home. We've got exactly two BattleMechs on the entire planet, and they're spoken for."

Will shook his head. "I don't want to be a MechWarrior," he said—and it was true. He'd always failed to understand the attraction of the giant fighting machines. Big as they were, next to the mountains they were small. "I just want to enlist."

Ap Rhys's expression became somewhat friendlier. "Then we might have a place for you." He gestured at the chair facing him. "Sit down, and let's talk."

Will sat down. Ap Rhys produced a sheaf of papers and a pen from the top drawer of his desk.

"Now, then," the Master Sergeant said. "Full name?"

"William Alan Elliot."

"Place and date of birth?"

"Harlaugh General Hospital. 3109."

"Education?"

"Liddisdale Secondary School," he said. "3127."

Master Sergeant ap Rhys gave him a considering look. "You're a bit older than the usual run of walk-ins we get here. Do you have a current employer?"

Will shook his head. "That's why I'm here."

"I see," the Master Sergeant said. "What about your previous employer?"

"Rockhawk Wilderness Tours. I was a guide."

"What was the reason for your discharge?"

"There wasn't enough work left for two guides," Will said. "I was the spare."

The Master Sergeant looked sympathetic. "Things like that can happen when times are bad. So you want to move from being a guide to being a soldier."

"I have to work at something. And soldiering must be better than working at the lumber mill."

"We'll see if you still feel that way four years from now," the Master Sergeant said. He pulled another document out of the collection from his desk, and marked one of the blank spaces near the bottom with a scrawled X. "If you'll sign here, we can start with the preliminary swearing in and move right on into the standard test battery. That'll give us an idea what your best assignment is going to be."

He paused and looked Will in the eye. "If you're going to back out, now's the time and the door to the street is right behind you. Once you've signed—hunting down a deserter is a deal of trouble."

Everything was suddenly moving very fast, Will thought. The pen was slippery in his hand; he managed to write "Will Elliot" in the indicated blank without scrawling too badly, but it was a near thing.

"Now," said Master Sergeant ap Rhys. "Raise your right hand and repeat after me: I, state your name, do solemnly swear—"

"I, William Alan Elliot, do solemnly swear—"

"That I will support and defend The Republic of the Sphere—"

"That I will support and defend The Republic of the Sphere," Will echoed.

"And I will obey the orders of the Exarch and the orders of the officers appointed over me, according to law and regulations."

Will experienced a sudden desire to put down his hand and run from the office. He fought it off and continued, somewhat shakily, "And I will obey the orders of the Exarch and the orders of the officers appointed over me, according to law and regulations."

"Now the Regiment owns your sorry ass for the next four years," said Master Sergeant Dylan ap Rhys. "On your feet, soldier, and go out through the other door—you have some tests to take."

9

The Fort
City of Tara, Northwind
December, 3132; local winter

Colonel Michael Griffin arrived at the Fort shortly after dark on the night of the Regimental reception for Paladin Ezekiel Crow. As he approached the main entrance to the complex, he could not help but feel a certain amount of pride in a job well done. In the short time available, the Northwind Highlanders had pulled together an impressive display in honor of their distinguished guest. Colored lights played over the structure's rugged exterior, bathing it in festive splashes of blue and red and green. The windows, high up on the massive walls, shone yellow with the light from inside.

A steady stream of vehicles came and went at the front gate, dropping off prominent politicians, high-ranking Regimental officers, prominent offworlders resident on Northwind, and representatives of the planet's most prominent families and most important business interests: Everyone, in short, who merited an introduction to the newly arrived Paladin, or who—regardless of merit—might consider himself fatally insulted without one. Security would be unobtrusive but omnipresent. The dress-uniformed soldiers standing guard at the entrance would not be so crass as to demand identification of the arriving guests, but no one who lacked an invitation would be admitted to the festivities. Those invitations—as Griffin, who'd assisted with their design, had good reason to know—were as individualized and personal as an ID card and a great deal harder to forge.

He showed his own invitation to the guards, exchanged salutes with them, and made his way up through all the levels of the Fort to the grand reception hall. At one end of the long, high-ceilinged room, a chamber orchestra played music from the prespaceflight days of Terra. The soft chords and rippling arpeggios ran like a melodious undercurrent through the murmur of conversation. Behind a long table at the other end of the hall, and at smaller tables placed at intervals along both sides, caterers in formal dress stood ready to serve the guests with food and drink. The long table had a towering ice sculpture of a *Blade* BattleMech for a centerpiece. Griffin gave the caterers points for quick and thorough intelligence gathering if not for subtlety: Ezekiel Crow had brought a *Blade* with him to Northwind.

The Paladin himself stood with Tara Campbell at the base of one of the hall's tall lancet windows, far enough from the music that his conversation with those who were introduced to him would not be overpowered. The window was also far enough from any of the refreshment tables that those guests who had come specifically to meet Ezekiel Crow would not be jostled by all the other guests who had come to fulfill an obligation to be present and who—having been counted among those attending—now desired only to sample the decorative pastries and the sparkling punch, and go home.

Years of attending regimental and diplomatic bun-fights all over Northwind and most of Prefecture III had made Griffin an expert in the art of juggling cup, napkin, and plate of small edible objects without risk to his dress uniform. Secure in the knowledge that one more regimental officer with his hands full of refreshments would not draw anyone's attention, he withdrew to one side of the reception hall and watched the Countess and the Paladin from a discreet distance.

Griffin had seen numerous photographic images and tri-vid clips of Ezekiel Crow, but this reception marked the first time he'd had an opportunity to observe the man in person. Crow was not a physically imposing man. Like most of those who successfully trained as MechWarrior, he was of little more than average height, but he had an undeniable presence. His dark brown hair and reserved demeanor made him an effective foil to the Countess's platinum-haired ebullience, and to Griffin's trained eye he carried himself as a man schooled to fight in numerous disciplines.

Tara Campbell stood in vibrant contrast to the more somber Paladin. She'd chosen to wear formal civilian garb tonight, a long, full-skirted gown of rich black velvet and a tartan sash pinned at her shoulder with a massive amber brooch, and she'd done something to her short blond hair—Griffin couldn't tell what—that had smoothed out its aggressive spikiness into a gleaming helmet that emphasized the elegant lines of her neck. Dressed so, she looked very much like the Countess of Northwind, and very little like the battle-tested MechWarrior, heroine of the campaign against the Black Dragon pirates on Sadalbari.

Griffin reminded himself that appearances could be deceiving, and that the petite porcelain Countess had been the martial-arts champion of the Northwind Military Academy during her student days. Her gown's long sleeves and full skirts would be hiding not soft flesh but firm muscle, and her grace of movement was a fighter's grace.

He had watched the Paladin and the Countess long enough, he decided. It was time to make his official appearance and pay his respects. He set his empty glass and plate aside on one of the side trays provided for the purpose, and moved to join the small throng of guests waiting their turn for a minute or two of talk with the reception's guest of honor.

When Tara Campbell saw him, she gave him a smile of genuine recognition and not mere practiced politeness, then turned, still smiling, to Ezekiel Crow.

"My lord, you really must meet the man who helped plan so much of this evening," she said to the Paladin. "Paladin Ezekiel Crow, may I present Colonel Michael Griffin of the First Gurkhas?"

Crow was in uniform, as was Griffin, and the two men exchanged salutes. From this closer vantage point, Griffin saw that Crow's eyes were not brown or hazel, as the color of his hair might have indicated. They were, in fact, dark blue. Griffin found the mismatch subtly off-putting, for reasons that he could not clearly articulate. Tara Campbell also had blue eyes, but her fair complexion and platinum hair gave them a more appropriate setting.

"Colonel Griffin," Crow said. His voice was low-pitched, and free of any planetary accent that Griffin could identify. Maybe such blandness was a requirement for anyone who intended to play Republic politics at the Paladin level, but Griffin couldn't help thinking that he'd prefer to hear an honest touch of local patois in a man's voice. "It's an honor to meet you tonight."

"I'm equally honored, my lord," said Griffin. "Under the present circumstances, it takes a brave and committed man to risk travel to another planet for the sake of nothing but the chance of danger and hard work."

"I go where The Republic of the Sphere sees fit to send me," Crow replied. "Which, for now, is Northwind."

Tara Campbell gave Crow another smile. To Griffin's eyes her expression appeared slightly apologetic, as if she might be remembering her earlier ambivalence about the Paladin and his mission to Prefecture III.

"And we're all grateful," she said. "Once these formalities are over, we can get down to work on the real issues." She looked around the vast reception hall and added, "Under somewhat less crowded circumstances, of course. Out of all these people, I think I see perhaps half a dozen who might actually need to be in the loop. Maybe fewer."

"You and I, of course," Crow said. "The Planetary Legate. The Governor. Colonel Griffin, will you be there as well?"

"I've found that the Colonel wears many hats," Tara Campbell said. Griffin couldn't tell from her expression and tone of voice whether she meant to counter the Paladin's subtle dig or simply to state a fact. "One of them is Prefect's liaison with the local intelligence networks. So we'll definitely need him on the team."

"It will be my pleasure," said Michael Griffin.

10

The Fort
City of Tara, Northwind
December, 3132; local winter

Tara Campbell was pleased to see that in spite of the last-minute nature of the operation, the Regimental reception for Paladin Ezekiel Crow was going smoothly. For a combat officer with a sideline in domestic intelligence, Colonel Michael Griffin had turned out to be surprisingly good at pulling a party together. She made a mental note to write him up a letter of commendation; as her father had said more than once, it never hurt to have another one or two of those in your personnel file, as a reserve against later disaster.

In the meantime, she intended to take advantage of her first opportunity to spend any length of time with the newly arrived Paladin. She still felt somewhat irked that the Exarch had placed so little confidence in her, but the irritation was tempered with a profound relief that she was not, after all, going to have to face everything that was coming alone.

And if she had to work with a Paladin of the Sphere, she had to admit that Ezekiel Crow was one of the best: distinguished graduate of the military academy right here on Northwind; Planetary Legate for Footfall in Prefecture V; leader of a successful campaign against smuggling and terrorist activity in that region; Knight of the Sphere; architect of a peaceful settlement to the Liao Conservatory of Military Arts Rebellion; and finally, a Paladin at the young—for that position—age of forty.

She wasn't certain what she'd expected, as far as appearance went. She'd seen occasional pictures and tri-vee likenesses of him, and while they gave the viewer an idea of things like height and coloring, and recorded his fondness for wearing civilian clothing of plain color and conservative cut on those rare occasions when he wasn't in uniform, they did nothing to convey his undeniable presence.

Crow had chosen to wear dress uniform that night—making it the first time that many of the guests at the reception had seen a Paladin in all of his glory. Tara was glad that she'd decided to wear formal civilian clothing, which wouldn't threaten to outshine him. The plain black velvet gown made an effective contrast to the richness of Crow's military regalia.

Alone among the guests, Colonel Griffin had seemed less than completely overawed by Ezekiel Crow. He'd been perfectly respectful, of course, just . . . standoffish, in a way that he had never been while working with Tara alone. Perhaps he too had felt insulted on her behalf by the Exarch's gift. If so, she could hardly fault his loyalty.

Everybody else, on the other hand, had professed themselves delighted to meet the Paladin. Tara watched with appreciation as Crow greeted the president of the Northwind branch of Bannson Universal Unlimited, talked economics with him earnestly for three minutes, and sent the man on his way smiling.

At the next lull in the conversation, she murmured, "Damn, my lord, but you're good. I couldn't have handled him that neatly if I'd tried."

His answering smile warmed the dark blue of his eyes, and softened his austere features into something close to attractiveness. "I've had considerably more practice."

"It's the part of political life I like the least," she admitted. "Pretending to be interested in everybody. I suppose I'm just a soldier at heart, like my father."

"You could do worse. Everything I've heard about Jon Campbell says that he was a good man."

"He was," she said. "It's been years, now, and I still miss him." She forced a smile. "But enough of past hurts. Can I offer you some whisky punch, my lord?"

He shook his head. "Your local recipes are too strong for me, I'm afraid. I don't drink."

"Try some of the pink fizzy stuff, then. It's guaranteed free of intoxicating or hallucinogenic substances." She caught the eye of a member of the catering staff. "Bring the Paladin a glass of the offworlders' punch and a plate of the mixed pastries, please."

She turned back to Crow. "We don't want you expiring from hunger before we have a chance to pick your brains and use your expertise."

"I'll do my best to stay alive, then, and ready for the picking."

It was hard to tell in the atmospheric lighting of the reception hall—myriad small faux candles in the crystal chandeliers overhead, and dozens of larger ones in the mirror-backed sconces along the wall—but she thought that she saw him color slightly as soon as the words came out. She was surprised. She'd thought that a Paladin would be above noticing such accidental double meanings, let alone committing them.

Apparently not, she thought, blushing a little herself, and hastened to change the subject. "I foresee a deal of boredom in your future, my lord. Everybody from the Planetary Legate down to the cooks is going to be lined up to ask you what's what and how are they doing it this year back on Terra."

"Not the cooks, surely." His plate of delicacies had arrived, and he was making considerable inroads into the smoked finny serpent in pastry, the candied fruits, and the little cakes with the nut toppings. "I haven't had some of these dishes since my student days here. I'm guessing that all of the ingredients are local?"

"Yes." His words gave her an idea. She turned it over in her head a couple of times, then said, "We'll have to schedule at least a few of your many, many meetings for an afternoon in Castle Northwind. The cooks will be put on their mettle by the chance to show off."

"Castle Northwind is your family's principal residence?"

"Yes," she said. "I live here in the city these days, but Castle Northwind is where I did most of my growing up. The staff will be delighted if I bring them home something as exotic as a Paladin."

"By all means, then, let us give your staff a treat."

Tara found herself blushing again. She was not completely inexperienced—she could hardly be that, after getting her schooling in the intense and often sexually charged atmosphere of the Northwind Military Academy—but in all of her half-formed fantasies and daydreams, she'd never visualized herself in such casual, almost flirtatious, conversation with a Paladin of the Sphere.

Don't even think of it, she told herself. *He outranks you politically and militarily both, he's a guest on your world and—very soon now—in your family home, and he's quite probably been sent out from Terra for the express purpose of either keeping you from making disastrous mistakes or reporting back to the Exarch when you do. No good could possibly come from a romantic entanglement with this man.*

She would have to be careful around Paladin Ezekiel Crow.

11

Camp Jaffray
Northwind
January, 3133; local summer

The summer sun was setting over the plains of western Halidon as the bus groaned and settled to a halt. Will Elliot looked out at the sprawling assortment of dusty redbrick buildings and saw a man approaching the bus on foot. He was dressed in a sharply pressed uniform of Northwind drab, and so far as Will could determine, he was alone.

The doors at the front and rear of the bus sighed open, and the man spoke. "All right, sweethearts, off the bus. Move it!" He had to have lungs of iron, Will thought, to make the words penetrate.

"Move, move, move," the man chanted. His voice carried through the sides of the bus as if the vehicle had been made of paper rather than of steel and glass.

Will stood and joined the other recruits moving toward the exits. The rear exit was closer; he headed that way, going with the crowd and taking the steps at a fast shuffling pace.

The parking lot outside the bus was flat black macadam, without so much as a sprig of grass growing through a crack—if there had been cracks, which was not the case. The pavement was so meticulously maintained that nothing marred its smooth perfection. Even the red dust which seemed so much a part of the surrounding landscape had apparently been swept away. Somebody, thought Will, must work hard to keep the surface in such good order.

On the pavement ahead of him was a set of footprints, painted in yellow. The footprints met at the heels, a forty-five-degree angle leading away toward the toes. They faced away from the bus.

"On your marks, people," the sharply pressed man said. "You're wasting my time. You don't want to waste my time."

He wasn't raising his voice, Will realized. He was speaking with no audible strain, but nevertheless punching the sounds out so that they could be clearly heard by everyone. Will moved forward with the rest of the new recruits until he found an unoccupied set of painted footprints. Then he stood, centering his feet in the outlines, and waited. He was in the second row from the front, near the right-hand side.

Behind him, Will heard the wheeze and rumble of the bus starting up and pulling away. He was aware of his fellow travelers, fifty young men and women counting himself, shifting uneasily on their marks. He didn't turn to look, or gaze around.

The sharply pressed man paced back and forth in front of the group. At last he looked at his watch, and turned toward them. His gaze ran up and down the ranks of waiting recruits, meeting each one's eyes. Then he spoke again, in the same carrying voice.

"Good evening, gentlemen and ladies. I am Master Sergeant O'Neill. This is Camp Jaffray. You are recruits. Right now none of you has a birthday. If you work hard and do as you are told, it is possible that someday the Regiment of Northwind may issue you a birthday. Now. 'Ten–SHUN!"

The last word cracked out hard enough that Will nearly jumped. Instead, he tried to stand straighter.

"People, that is pathetic. The position of attention is as follows. Your feet are together, toes pointing slightly out. Your hands fall to your sides, palms toward your legs. Your thumb lies in the groove between your first two fingers, and along the outer seams of your trousers. Your stomach is in, your chest is out, you are gazing straight forward. This is a very comfortable position. When called to attention, you remain in that position until some other order is given. Take this as a general rule: When given an order, you will carry out that order until given another order."

Master Sergeant O'Neill fell silent, and resumed his pacing. He passed out of Will's line of sight. Will remained in place. The sky grew darker. Lights on towers switched on, bathing the tarmac in white light that made the shadows seem deeper. After what seemed like hours, he heard another voice, as loud as O'Neill's had been.

"Good evening, Master Sergeant O'Neill."

"Good evening, Master Sergeant Murray," O'Neill replied.

"What do you have for me?"

"A gaggle of civilians," O'Neill said. "No help for it, I suppose."

"One or two of them might make soldiers," Murray said. "May I have them?"

"With pleasure," O'Neill said. Then: "People, this is Master Sergeant Murray. He will discover which of you is meant to have the honor of fighting for Northwind. If he says jump, you don't ask how high. You jump and hope it's high enough."

Another long pause followed. Then Murray's voice: "Recruits! Left face!"

Will turned to his left. He was looking up a long row of men and women, though he couldn't see much through the head of the man in front of him.

"No hope," O'Neill said, still projecting his voice.

"Perhaps not," Murray said. "People. In a

moment I will say, 'Forward, march.' 'Forward' is a preparatory command. A preparatory command tells you what is to come. 'March' is a command of execution. When a command of execution is given, you will perform the action for which you have been prepared. In this case, to march forward. Very simple. Even recruits can do it."

Murray's voice was moving down the line to Will's left; the man himself was out of Will's line of sight. "On the command 'march,' you will step forward with your left foot. Then with your right foot. Then with your left. Every foot should strike the ground at the same instant. You will continue in this manner until another command is given."

The voice was moving behind Will now. Ahead, but quite a distance away, stood another of the brick buildings, its windows brightly lighted.

"The next command, tonight, will be 'Ready, halt.' 'Ready' will be the preparatory command. 'Halt' will be the command of execution. On the word 'halt' your left foot will strike the ground; then your right foot will come up beside it, and you will once again be in the position of attention."

The voice was moving up to the right, and Will caught sight of the Master Sergeant out of the corner of his eye. A short man, Will thought, though with wide shoulders. The Master Sergeant came up to the corner of the column and turned to face the men. "Forward," he said. "March."

Will stepped out with his left foot, and attempted to keep lined up with the men to his right and left, while following the man in front of him.

"Left, left, left, right, left," Murray shouted. "Keep it together, recruits. This is not an amble along the riverbank with your sweetheart." Will felt the foot of the man behind him come down on his heel. He stumbled a bit; that hurt.

"Left, right, left. One, two, three, four, left."

Will counted to himself, along with the Sergeant. This was no great thing; he'd walked farther than this every day of his life. It was only the keeping in step that was different. The building ahead grew nearer, and Will could see now that they were heading toward it. Its wide double doors stood open, and yellow light poured out from the interior.

"Company!" Murray shouted. "Ready, halt! One, two."

They were facing directly into the open doors.

"I will call you off by files," Master Sergeant Murray said. "When I do so, you will follow the red lines painted on the floor. You will come to a number of stations. You will be given instructions. Follow them. You have no cause to talk to anyone. Now. Company. At ease!"

He paused for a moment. " 'At ease' is yet another order. It means 'you may move your right foot, though your left will remain in one place as if glued there. You will clasp your hands in the small of your back. You may look around, but you may not talk.' Try it again. Company! At ease!"

Will clasped his hands in the small of his back, as instructed, and waited for the command that would send him into the open building and the next phase of his strange new life.

PART TWO

Tigress, Summer 3133
Power Play

12

DropShip Landing Field
The Four Cities, Tigress
Prefecture IV, Republic of the Sphere
April, 3133; local summer

On Tigress, the day was clear and dazzlingly bright. The air above the landing field rippled with midsummer heat. Then ground and air alike trembled with a heavy, growling vibration as an object came into view in the sky above the field: first a dot, then a disk, then a huge and steadily descending shape, as the first of the DropShips landed with a roar and rumble. The Steel Wolves were coming home to the Four Cities.

The fighting had been good on Achernar, at least for those of the Wolves who had won honor and promotion. Not everybody was happy among those returning. Some of the Warriors looked beyond the fighting to the longer strategy, and saw Achernar still master of its own fate, loyal to The Republic of the Sphere and controlled neither by the Steel Wolves nor by Lord Aaron Sandoval and his puppet Erik Sandoval-Groell. The defenders of Achernar could boast that they had taken on Kal Radick's Steel Wolves and sent them home bleeding, and that was no little thing in times like these.

Star Colonel Anastasia Kerensky saw the longer strategy as well as anybody else. Nevertheless, she had a bit of a swagger in her step as she left the DropShip *Lupus,* with her leather jacket slung over her shoulder and the sun picking up the red highlights in her thick black hair.

The patches and blazons on the jacket told an interesting story. Its wearer, they said, had indeed fought in the campaign just past, but her fellow Warriors had not been Clan. Anastasia grinned, remembering. She'd had fun on Achernar, fighting next to the locals and testing herself against Kal Radick's Steel Wolves. Finding a comrade-in-arms—and a pleasing if temporary lover—in her fellow MechWarrior Raul Ortega. Being Tassa Kay.

The grin faded a little. Raul Ortega had gone back to his local woman in the end, and Tassa Kay was—not dead, exactly, but put away until the next time Anastasia wanted to shed for a little while the ambitions and expectations that went with being the bearer of a famous Bloodname. And there was no Bloodname more famed among the Clans than Kerensky.

Aleksandr and Nicholas Kerensky had pulled the ancestors of the Clans away from the wreckage of the original Star League and made them into what they now were. Natasha Kerensky, the Black Widow, had won fame and notoriety throughout the Inner Sphere as one of the group of mercenaries—and covert intelligence gatherers—called the Wolf's Dragoons. Anastasia, for her part, intended to take the Kerensky Bloodname still further before she was done.

For now, she needed to get herself established here on Tigress. The port workers could handle the offloading and berthing of her *Ryoken II* BattleMech without her direct supervision, and could begin the job of cleaning it up and repairing the damage it had taken during the campaign on Achernar. She would check up on their progress frequently, of course, because the *Ryoken II* was hers—her weapon and protection in battle, a metal-and-myomer extension of her physical self—and its continuing good condition was as important to her as her own. But Tigress was a Clan world now, and its port laborers and repair techs would know the difference between a real fighting machine and a retrofitted piece of industrial gear. Meanwhile, Anastasia had other work to do.

Her first stop was the Portmaster's office. The Portmaster, like the laborers who worked under him, was a Steel Wolf from one of the labor castes—in his case, from among those charged with administration and record keeping. His placid expression changed when she entered his office; she could see that he already knew who she was. Absolutely nothing travels faster than gossip, and Anastasia was well aware that the news had spread from the DropShip faster than its passengers could disperse: *A Kerensky is among us.*

"Star Colonel?" he asked.

His voice was deferential. His manner was not cringing or subservient—he was a Wolf, even if he was not a Warrior, and no Wolf was ever subservient—but he nevertheless accorded her the deference befitting her rank and name. She had missed that automatic deference while she was fighting among the natives on Achernar, even while Tassa Kay was enjoying the easy camaraderie that had filled its place.

She gave the man a brief nod of acknowledgment. "Portmaster," she said. "Is there anything happening at the moment here on Tigress that a new arrival ought to know?"

"Your arrival with the DropShips from Achernar is the only matter of current interest," the Portmaster said. "We have already arranged a local berthing facility for your *Ryoken II,* and a repair crew has been assigned."

A reputation, Anastasia reflected, was a handy thing to have, even if so far hers was mostly genetic and not of her own making.

"Excellent," she said.

"And for yourself, Star Colonel—do you wish your personal effects taken to Headquarters?"

Anastasia had done her research before embarking on this adventure. The newly constructed Headquarters building housed the senior Steel Wolf officers present on Tigress—at least, it would do so once the Wolves finished settling in—and her rank of Star Colonel entitled her to a substantial set of rooms.

"No," she said. "I plan to look for accommodation on the local economy."

A person could obtain a great deal more privacy by securing private housing, and could also escape the strain of having to endure the company of potential rivals on a round-the-clock basis. Living alone would also make it easier, if she ever wanted, to bring Tassa Kay out of hiding for a few hours of irresponsible fun.

"As the Star Colonel wishes," said the Portmaster. "The Four Cities area has a wide range of possibilities available for officers who want to look for separate quarters, and Headquarters keeps a list of recommended housing providers on file."

"Excellent. I would prefer not to waste good time looking at bad rooms." She gave him her best charismatic smile. It had worked for Tassa Kay on Achernar, and it would work again on Tigress for Anastasia Kerensky. Start with the support staff and go on from there, gaining their goodwill and admiration, or at least their respect. "Out in the field is one thing—all of us have seen worse than cold water and thin walls and the local vermin—but just because something can be endured on campaign is no reason anyone should consent to live with it afterwards."

"My feelings exactly, Star Colonel," the Portmaster said. "Aside from the berthing and repair of your BattleMech, is there anything else that you need?"

"One thing, yes," she said. "Inform Galaxy Commander Kal Radick that Star Colonel Anastasia Kerensky has arrived on Tigress, and that she wishes to meet with him at his earliest convenience."

13

Steel Wolf Headquarters
The Four Cities, Tigress
April, 3133; local summer

For Anastasia Kerensky, Kal Radick's earliest convenience came sooner than she had expected. She had spent most of her first day on Tigress combing through the local rental and purchase listings, tackling the acquisition of living quarters with a ruthlessness that left sales and rental agents exhausted. Her efforts brought their own reward: By late afternoon, she had the keys to a one-bedroom apartment in neither the best nor the worst section of the Four Cities. The building itself was an unattractive brick structure, like a shipping crate with windows, but it was well kept up by neighborhood standards, and its security systems were excellent.

And for all the building's laboring-class ugliness, it possessed one overwhelming advantage:

Nobody in the Steel Wolves would expect to find Star Colonel Anastasia Kerensky living in such a place. She still had Tassa Kay's mustering-out money from her service on Achernar, in good Republic stones—more than enough to cover her first and last month's rent and her security deposit, and to pay for the activation of utilities and a connection to the planetary communications net. All done with the pleasant anonymity of cash.

Privacy, she thought. And cheap at the price. She hoped that hard currency would continue in use on Clan worlds in the Republic. If the Steel Wolves ever managed to reestablish the standard Clan voucher system locally, such anonymity would be much more difficult to come by.

She checked the net connection on the spot by locating and opening her official mail. Nothing there . . . except for a note asking for the pleasure of her company at dinner that evening with Galaxy Commander Kal Radick.

"Fast work," she said aloud, and didn't bother to explain her comment to the rental agent. Radick obviously wanted to meet her before she had a chance to settle in—wanted to catch her on the run and see what she was like with her guard down. "Well, the hell with *that*."

Her personal gear was still back at the DropShip field; she hadn't wanted to haul a full duffel all over the city while looking at apartments. But her earlier cordiality toward the Portmaster proved to have been a good investment.

Upon her return, he proved willing to let her clean up and change into uniform in the female employees' locker room.

"I do not want to keep Galaxy Commander Radick waiting," she explained as she collected her duffel and headed for the showers. When she reemerged a few minutes later, scrubbed clean and freshly dress-uniformed, Tassa Kay was gone completely and the Star Colonel was ascendant.

Public transport took her to the Headquarters building where Kal Radick had his quarters—no living off base for him.

"Star Colonel Kerensky to see Galaxy Commander Radick," she said to the guard at the front entrance. "I am expected."

The guard consulted his data pad. "You will find his quarters on the top floor, Star Colonel. Take the elevator up and follow the signs for Twenty-Five A through F."

She was not surprised, when she reached her destination, to find Kal Radick's rooms austere almost to point of bareness: stark metal-and-crystal furniture, with the walls and carpet and curtains done in shades of brown and gray and bone ivory. The Clan aesthetic sense ran to the purely functional in matters of design, even when the materials themselves, as here, were the best available. Anastasia Kerensky, trueborn of the iron wombs on Arc-Royal, approved, but the voice of Tassa Kay whispered impudently in the back of her mind that some people might consider that the Galaxy Commander was trying a bit too hard.

Radick himself was a lean man, on the tall side for a MechWarrior, with dark hair and a complexion either deep tanned or naturally olive. He came forward to greet her at the door.

"Star Colonel Kerensky," he said.

He sounded genuinely pleased by her arrival, and Anastasia had to remind herself that the Galaxy Commander was younger than he looked. His true age didn't show in his appearance or in his general bearing, but she had delved into the history behind his meteoric rise to the rank of Prefect. Mixed in with the triumphs—his gaining of the Radick Bloodname, his successful challenge for the position of Galaxy Commander for the Clan Clusters in Prefecture IV—she had seen other, more disquieting things.

His dealings with the new Prefect of Prefecture III, for example. Kal Radick clearly had no idea how much he had offended the Countess of Northwind by his suggestion that The Republic of the Sphere might eventually be replaced by a renascent Star League. The Campbell woman was passionately loyal to Devlin Stone's Republic. Anastasia, for her part, found such passion for a jerry-built political experiment more amusing than anything else—and had reacted to Kal Radick's offhand comment as though he had spoken deliberate treason.

If the Countess of Northwind had been Clan, Anastasia thought, we would have had a Trial of Grievance by now, and the whole Inner

Sphere would have learned which side had the stronger argument.

All this passed through her mind as she weighed the proper response to Kal Radick's greeting. The tone of the evening was social, rather than official—their meeting was in private quarters rather than in public space, and food and drink were on offer—but not too social, since Radick wore a plain working uniform rather than civilian clothing.

Anastasia settled for making eye contact and giving Radick a nod in reply. "Galaxy Commander Radick."

"Have you eaten?" he asked.

"Breakfast this morning only," she said. "I have been occupied with settling in."

Radick gestured toward the table she had glimpsed earlier. It stood in a window nook overlooking the DropPort. Night was falling outside, but the silhouettes of *Lupus* and its mates were still visible on the landing field. "Join me, then."

"Happily, Galaxy Commander."

The meal that waited for them turned out to be much like the room it was served in: everything of the best quality, but all of it plain to the point of simplicity. Not ostentatiously so—the Galaxy Commander did not dine at home on field rations, or on anything badly cooked or otherwise inedible—but bland and unsophisticated nonetheless. She wondered if the near austerity was meant as a political gesture, to demonstrate to the more militant among the

Steel Wolves that he was uncorrupted by the ways of The Republic in spite of having been immersed in its politics.

"What brings you to Prefecture IV?" Radick asked. He filled his plate with sliced roast meat and boiled greens as he spoke. "Tigress is a long way from Arc-Royal, quaiff?"

In more ways than one, she thought. "Aff."

"Yet you came here by way of Achernar. Why?"

Anastasia began filling her own plate. After not having had a chance to eat since leaving the DropShip that morning, even plain meat and greens were going to taste good.

"The DropPort on Achernar makes a convenient stopover point," she said. "Or do you mean—why did I fight beside the locals while I was there?"

"That question is also one that requires an answer."

"Perhaps," she said, "I desired to see for myself what the famous Steel Wolves were made of."

"And did you?"

She gave him a quick, predatory grin, feeling for a moment more Tassa Kay than Anastasia Kerensky. "Oh, yes."

"I trust you found it satisfactory."

"Had what I seen not pleased me, I would not have continued on to Tigress afterward."

Radick looked satisfied by the answer, and Anastasia Kerensky allowed herself another, more inward smile. She had no intention of explaining to the Galaxy Commander exactly what she had found pleasing: the knowledge that the Steel Wolves were strong enough and hard enough to be made into a sword that could break apart The Republic of the Sphere; but more than that, the knowledge that Kal Radick would not be the one to use them.

14

Kal Radick's Headquarters
The Four Cities, Tigress
April, 3133; local summer

Anastasia Kerensky's first opportunity to test the mettle of Kal Radick's Steel Wolves from the commanding, rather than the opposing, side came within a week of her arrival on Tigress. The Wolves were planning a strike against the planet Ruchbah in Prefecture III, ostensibly to gain control of an additional source of civilian and military vehicles. It was clear to Anastasia, however, that the primary purpose of the strike was to test the strength and fighting will of The Republic in Prefecture III.

It was also possible, Anastasia reflected as she made her way from her apartment to Headquarters through the morning Four Cities traffic, that Kal Radick wanted to give his warriors an easy victory, to lift the spirits of those who had noticed that the fighting on Achernar had provided them with nothing of the sort. She laughed aloud at the thought—better to give the Wolves a true challenge and let them beat it, in her opinion—and the other occupants of the municipal hovertransport looked at her oddly but said nothing. A Star Colonel, even one who lived on the edge of the rough part of town and relied on public transit to get about, was entitled to laugh at whatever happened to strike her as amusing.

When she reached the Headquarters building, she made herself known to the guard at the door. Then she proceeded to the main strategy room, where the upcoming batchall—the bidding before combat—was slated to take place. The Galaxy Commander himself was not yet in evidence, but a quick glance around the room showed that it was already full of his supporters. She recognized Star Colonels Ulan and Marks, currently two of the highest in Radick's esteem. A number of Star Captains and Star Commanders stood among the group of uniformed men and women gathered around the central map table, but they would most likely be only spectators, come to observe the batchall and take their initial measure of the leader they would have to serve under in the upcoming campaign.

The lower-ranked officers made way for Anastasia as she moved through the crowd to take a place at the perimeter of the map table. The table's surface was divided at the moment into two displays, one showing the overall topography of Ruchbah, and the other the streets and buildings of the capital city. Star Colonel Ulan looked at her suspiciously; Marks ignored her. Anastasia said nothing to either Warrior.

The door of the strategy room opened to admit Galaxy Commander Kal Radick, then closed again. Radick came up to the table and announced, "Trothkin, the Wolves are bound for glory, and that path currently leads us to the world of Ruchbah. Let all who would join in that glory step forward for the batchall in this Trial of Possession for the Michaelson Industries plant."

A cluster of buildings on the city map lit up in yellow as Radick spoke.

"The cut-down for the bidding is two Trinaries," he continued, "each Trinary to be composed of five 'Mechs, ten vehicles, and armored and unarmored infantry. Let none who would not achieve victory participate. Who will bid first?"

Star Colonel Marks spoke first. "I bid a Cluster."

A Cluster—three full Trinaries—was a good bid, though not an especially daring one. It was well above the cut-down set by Radick as the minimum amount of force needed to achieve the objective. Marks was no fool; he had been among those officers who came away from Achernar less than happy with the outcome of that campaign. He had drawn lessons from the experience, it seemed; though not necessarily the best ones.

"Star Colonel Marks bids a full Cluster," said Radick. "Is there a lower bid?"

"I bid two Trinaries and a Star," Anastasia said. She saw the spectators begin exchanging glances. They must not have expected a newcomer like herself to enter the bidding, even though her rank gave her the right to do so if she chose.

Radick himself looked startled by her bid, but the change of expression was a fleeting one and he hid it well. If she had not already expected that Radick might find her participation in the batchall disturbing, she might not have noticed it at all.

"Star Colonel Anastasia Kerensky bids two Trinaries and a Star," Radick said. "Is there a lower bid?"

Star Colonel Ulan took a step closer to the table. "I bid two Trinaries less a 'Mech and five vehicles."

A ripple of surprise—not sound so much as hastily suppressed fractional movement, raised eyebrows and temporarily halted breaths and almost-invisible muscular twitches—ran through the assembled spectators. Bidding below cut-down was a daring move. If Star Colonel Ulan could not accomplish the objective with the original force, and had to call for reinforcements, he risked a considerable loss of honor.

"Star Colonel Marks?" Radick said.

Marks shook his head. "I have no further bid."

"Star Colonel Anastasia Kerensky?"

"I bid two Trinaries less two 'Mechs and seven vehicles."

"Star Colonel Anastasia Kerensky bids two Trinaries less two 'Mechs and seven vehicles. Star Colonel Ulan?"

Ulan cast a dark look in Anastasia's direction and said, "I bid two Trinaries less a Star."

The room fell quiet as Radick's officers waited to see how the newcomer from Arc-Royal would react to Ulan's bid.

Anastasia herself did not find the idea of bidding deep below cut-down inherently distasteful as some did. On the other hand, the cut-down, when properly set, functioned to prevent the waste of Clan resources in fruitless battle. In her judgment, Radick had set this raid's cut-down at an eminently reasonable level. On this occasion, she had been willing to go more than a bit under—Radick had, if anything, erred on the side of caution—but Ulan's last bid had been recklessly low.

"I have no further bid," she said.

Let Ulan have this raid, she thought. Losing honor through her own stupidity did not play any part in Anastasia Kerensky's long-term plan.

15

Kerensky residence
The Four Cities, Tigress
May, 3133; local summer

Anastasia Kerensky stalked into her apartment, wishing that the closing mechanism on the door would allow her to slam it. She yanked the bottle of vodka from the freezer, poured herself a tall glass and knocked it back. Imported Terran vodka, the real thing, a shame to waste that way—but she was a bearer of the Kerensky Bloodname and she would do as she damned well pleased. Terra's fruits of vine and field should have been hers anyway.

It was all meant to be ours, she thought. The Star League—the true Star League, not this cobbled-together latecomer called The Republic of the Sphere—was what the Clans had been created to restore and to serve, after all the rest of humanity had abandoned the ideal. People were fools if they thought that the mission had been abandoned just because some part of the Clans had accepted, for a while, the words of Devlin Stone.

Kal Radick had listened to those words. Kal Radick said now that he had forgotten them, and claimed that he was trying to lift the Steel Wolf Warriors back up to their former glory. As if he'd know a real Clan Wolf Warrior on sight.

Anastasia Kerensky poured another shot of vodka and slammed it back.

Kal Radick did not speak the truth.

If he were truly interested in taking back Terra, she thought, he would stop sabotaging her efforts during the batchall. Three times now, he had set the cut-down for the bidding cautiously high, encouraging his favorites to bid below the mark. Twice it had worked, if barely—both times, the leaders had needed to call for reinforcements to achieve their objectives, and had suffered no loss of their commander's good opinion thereby. Kal Radick had continued to allow them to bid in the batchalls, and had allowed—one might even say, had encouraged—them to undercut Anastasia's own bid every time.

This time, Kal Radick's policy had led not just to embarrassment, but to disaster—defeat and humiliation, ending in a retreat to the DropShips and a run back home, on a world that she, Anastasia Kerensky, could have taken with no BattleMechs at all.

Anastasia knew the dark mood that had overtaken her. It made her dangerous, to herself as much as others, and made her liable to do rash things. The last time she had been in such a state of mind, she had ended up leaving Arc-Royal for The Republic. That decision had proved not so bad, in the long run—but it could have been bad, if her luck had been worse, or if the long DropShip passages had not given her the opportunity to stop and think and plan.

I need to work this off right now, she thought, before I do something stupid and ruin everything.

She looked about her apartment. She had chosen to live on her own outside the Clan enclave on Tigress for a reason. She had guessed it might come at some point to this. It was time to call on an expert at having the kind of fun that would ease her mind and burn away some of the physical need that threatened to push her off the true path.

It was time to bring out Tassa Kay.

Anastasia turned to her closet and found the clothes she needed. She laid them out on the bed, item by item: the black leather breeches, cut to fit snug against the skin; the black silk shirt; the black leather jacket with its patches from Dieron and Achernar; the boots, polished black leather rising up past the knee.

And one more thing—a knife in its sheath, designed to be hidden up her sleeve. She had not needed the knife on Achernar, among comrades-in-arms; and she would have scorned to wear it on Tigress, among the Wolves. But the knife had come in handy more than once on the journey from Arc-Royal, and Tassa Kay liked it very much.

She dressed quickly, then left her apartment and headed for the Strip. Every DropPort had a Strip, regardless of what name the district might actually carry. It was the part of town where the entertainment establishments stood open all night and all day, where there were always bright lights and loud music, and where the law walked carefully if it entered at all. The Strip was full of places to spend money and blow off the mingled tension and boredom of long DropShip passages.

One would not—most of the time—find top-ranked Clan Warriors in places like that; only—sometimes—Clan members from the other castes, and non-Clan citizens and transients. And if one went looking for it, one could find trouble.

Anastasia Kerensky found a barroom. It had a garish multicolored facade, all pulsing lights and pounding music. Pleased by the gaudy spectacle, she went in.

She didn't have to work her way through the crowd. It parted for her as soon as she stepped across the threshold. She went up to the bar, and similar magic made an empty place appear.

"Vodka," she said, before the bartender could speak.

"Yes, Star Colonel."

Damn, she thought. Even here they knew her. She tossed back her drink, and made to leave the cash for it on the bar.

"On the house, Star Colonel."

A wave of frustration washed over her. She pulled out more cash and laid it down. "Buy the house a round on me, then. Good night."

She turned and left. As she went, she heard the excited murmurs behind her . . . "Kerensky?" "Kerensky!" . . . and headed deeper into the back alleys of the Strip.

Anastasia found, at last, a dive. The building had no windows anymore—the windows it had once were now all bricked up. The sign over the door, in mostly burned-out lights, read: BUCKET OF BLOOD.

She had to elbow past a stubble-bearded thug in a greasy coverall to make it in through the door, and then push herself in between two other lowlifes to reach the bar. She was not the only female in the room; but she was the only one whose occupation was not immediately obvious. Of the other women, two of them wore DropShip workers' coveralls—they were a pair, it looked like, and smart enough to do their payday drunken revel on the buddy system—and the remaining three wore skintight skirts, mesh blouses, and body glitter. All five of them looked at her glossy leathers with surly resentment.

The bartender eyed her suspiciously. "What do you want?"

"Strong drink," she said. "Vodka."

"Pay first," said the bartender. "No tabs here."

She slapped money down onto the bar. "Tell me when this runs out. And give me a drink."

Hot breath stirred the hairs on the back of her neck, and she half-turned to see the man she had shoved coming in the door.

"Hey," he said, in angry tones. "Who do you think you are?"

She gave him a sweet smile. "The person who is drinking here," she said. She felt the adrenaline rising, and shifted her position and her balance to be ready when Big-and-Greasy made his move. "If you want to drink here, you will have to do something about it."

He gave her a truculent glare. "You better be careful. Talk to the wrong person like that, and somebody could get hurt."

But not him, apparently, not here and not now. He was backing down and moving away grumbling. *Damn.* She was really feeling it now, the angry reckless burn, and she had nothing to let it loose on. She downed the last of her vodka, swept the bar with a contemptuous gaze, and swaggered out.

Anastasia made it two blocks before the footsteps she heard behind her gathered enough courage to come at her in a rush. In a surge of wild fierce joy she spun around and stepped into it, the knife dropping into her hand and punching upward into the attacker's gut.

Big-and-Greasy, she thought. Bleeding out on the pavement. No surprise there.

A voice from the street ahead commented, "That was nice."

She looked at the speaker. He was young and dark-haired and muscular, his voice and his dress both Clan-but-not-quite—freeborn to a local, perhaps? In the light from the nearest streetlamp, he was smiling.

"I wasn't doing it to give you a show." She let her accent slide downward out of true Clan precision—she was Tassa Kay tonight, and Tassa suddenly had another need, as strong as the need for violence. "But if you *liked* it—"

The man's smile grew wider. "Oh, I did."

She smiled back at him, the corpse of Big-and-Greasy already cooling at her feet. "Then we can go back to my place and do some other things that you might like even more."

16

Kerensky residence
The Four Cities, Tigress
May, 3133; local summer

Anastasia Kerensky woke up in a much better mood than the one that had sent her out looking for trouble on the DropPort Strip. Daylight filtering in through the drawn curtains of her bedroom brought her to full awareness slowly and comfortably. Her muscles felt relaxed and pleasantly fatigued, and she was conscious of the warm weight of another person lying next to her. Full memory of the night before returned, and she smiled as she treated herself to a langourous, full-body stretch.

It was a damned good thing, she thought, that the bed had turned out to be a solid piece of furniture, and not a shoddy piece of work some local landlord had purchased on the cheap for a furnished rental unit. Otherwise, the two of them could have broken it, after the point where she had discovered that her partner for the evening—freeborn local or no—was strong enough that she had no need to worry about breaking him.

She rolled over to look at him, and saw that he was already awake and looking at her. In the daylight that made its way past the curtains, he was not quite as young as she had guessed in the streetlamp's glow, but still perhaps a year or so her junior. He was dark-skinned and muscular, in a pleasantly compact kind of way, with black hair cropped short and a nicely shaped skull underneath. He had surprisingly full lips, and his eyes were a dark brown, almost black, very lively and curious.

"Good morning," she said, and smiled at him. "After a very good night. Do you happen to have a name?"

He smiled back at her with a flash of strong white teeth, like a carnivore's. "Nicholas Darwin."

That was a local name, she thought, not Clan. She felt a slight disappointment. Locals could be fun, in their way, but they always had people they wanted to go back to, and work that they did not want to abandon. "Are you off one of the DropShips?"

He laughed. "No. I'm a tanker. Star Captain."

That was not so bad after all. She propped herself up on one elbow and drew a fingernail along the line of crisply curling hair that ran down the center of his chest. "Darwin is not a Clan Wolf name."

"It was—" his breath caught as her fingernail

slid downward "—my mother's family name. My father was a Wolf Clansman, or so she said, and the genetic tests agreed."

"Ah."

Her hand stilled, and she considered him for a long moment in the morning light. Not really a local, then. True, he was freeborn and only half Clan—not quite good enough, it seemed, to go all the way to win a Bloodname and earn the right to ride a 'Mech into battle. But nevertheless he was both pleasant to look at and pleasant to take to bed, and Star Captain was a good enough rank that she need not be ashamed.

She made her decision.

"My name is Anastasia Kerensky."

"I know," he said.

"What!" she exclaimed indignantly. She sat bolt upright, so that the sheet slid down off her body and crumpled around her hips. "You *knew*?"

He was laughing, damn him, and giving her an unrepentant grin. "I recognized you buying drinks for the Purple Light Bar and followed you out."

"You followed me out." She was still seething, although inwardly she had to admit that she had not exactly been keeping a low profile at the time. "Why?"

"Curiosity," he said. "You acted like you were looking for something, and I wanted to see if you found it." His expression turned reminiscent. "And you certainly did. The way you handled that guy in the street . . . remind me never to make you mad."

"You're coming real close right now," she said, but she let her accent slide downward into Tassa Kay's casual imprecision, to take the sting out of the threat. "But you're right, Nicholas Darwin. I did indeed find something that I was looking for."

She rolled out of bed, heedless of Nicholas Darwin's gaze, and went over to the closet and began pulling out clothes for the day. Uniform, this time, and working, not dress. "I had a question. I was looking for the answer. And I found it."

"Fortune-telling through personal violence? That is a new one."

"There are a great many liars in the universe," she told him. "But death and violence, in my experience, tend to tell the truth."

At some point the night before—she was not sure if it had happened during the fight in the alley or during the sex afterward—Anastasia Kerensky had achieved an enlightenment of sorts. She knew what she wanted—she had *always* known what she wanted—but she understood now that the subtle approach was not going to work. On the likes of Duke Aaron Sandoval, perhaps, or on the offspring of House Kurita—clever, subtle adversaries who could appreciate a well-turned ploy. But Kal Radick was not a subtle man.

She shut the closet door and headed out of the bedroom, carrying the clean uniform with her.

"Where are you going?" Nicholas Darwin said.

"Right now? To get washed and dressed. And after that, Headquarters. I have words to exchange with the Galaxy Commander."

17

Steel Wolf Headquarters
The Four Cities, Tigress
May, 3133; local summer

Anastasia Kerensky entered the Steel Wolves' strategic planning room unannounced and let the door shut behind her. She noted with satisfaction that Kal Radick was indeed where his aide had told her he would be; even better, the big, high-ceilinged room was packed with Kal Radick's trusted subordinates, Star Colonels Ulan and Marks, as usual, as well as other high-ranking Warriors of the Steel Wolves. The trivid map display filling the surface of the table in the center of the room confirmed her suspicion that she had walked in on yet another batchall. Based on the map, Small World was the latest planet chosen to be the target of the Wolves' concentration.

As soon as she had everyone's attention, she

strode up to the table, to a spot opposite Kal Radick. She gave herself a slow count of five to look at the map of Small World, then deliberately raised one eyebrow and nodded as if to herself. Only then did she look across the table and say to Radick, "I am glad to see that our reverses on Quentin have not daunted you."

To either side of her, in her peripheral vision, she could see Marks and Ulan shifting position slightly and looking at each other. Their uneasy reaction confirmed her guess that she had not even been supposed to be here for this bidding.

He ignores me, he cuts me out. Me, Anastasia Kerensky.

The realization added fire to her resolve; she felt anger now, as well as justification. She channeled that anger into a wealth of dubious scorn as she spoke to Radick again, "But . . . Small World?"

Galaxy Commander Radick regarded her with a look of dawning unease. He replied carefully, as befitted the circumstances, when he must know that she had some agenda of her own, but not yet what that agenda might be. "Star Colonel Kerensky, would you care to participate in the batchall?"

"No."

She saw him relax a little at her answer, and under the relaxation noted a flicker of what had to be carefully suppressed contempt. He said, "The Star Colonel may remain and observe the bidding if she chooses."

Anastasia smiled a little at Radick, just to unnerve him further. "I am not interested in observing the bidding."

That caused a whispered buzz of comment among the assembled officers. They looked from her to Radick and back again, aware like their commander that something was up, but not knowing what.

"Then what is your purpose in coming here?" Radick asked.

"I wish to declare a separate batchall at this time."

The blunt statement brought on another, louder buzz of comment. Anastasia pushed on. "I am bidding myself, and myself only, to fight against Kal Radick in a Trial of Possession."

This time, there was dead silence in the room for the space of several breaths. Then Radick spoke. "For which of my resources or possessions do you intend to challenge?"

"Your rank as Galaxy Commander. And leadership of the Steel Wolves."

"On what grounds?"

"On the grounds that they are yours and that I want them to be mine." She met his gaze across the map table, where the three-dimensional topography of Small World lay spread out between them. "We are Wolves, are we not—what more is needed?"

"Rank and position are not appropriate stakes for a Trial of Possession." Radick looked at her narrowly. "Judging by your own words, it seems that you intend a Trial of Grievance."

Anastasia kept her face unchanged with an

effort, though she could not keep her chin from lifting slightly in the face of Radick's insult and her shoulders going back. She had not anticipated so deft a counterchallenge.

If she were to fight a Trial of Grievance against Radick and win, she still would not have the rank and position that she desired. To obtain it, she would have to fight her way through a Trial of Position with all of Radick's other Star Colonels—who would almost certainly turn their attention to eliminating her, the outsider who had defeated a popular commander, before moving against each other.

And he insults me as well, she thought, implying that I am ignorant of proper tradition and protocol. He thinks that making me angry will make me stupid. Wrong, Kal Radick. It only makes me angry.

"You have done me no direct injury, Galaxy Commander. I have no Grievance." She was in motion again, stalking around the perimeter of the map table, ending—deliberately—just outside comfortable speaking distance with Radick. "You, on the other hand, have something that I want."

She took another two steps, which brought her well inside speaking distance. "And I believe that I am better suited than you to possess it."

Radick stood his ground. "How so?"

She pivoted and threw out an arm in a deliberately theatrical gesture, pointing to the map.

"Look at this!" Her voice was pitched to carry; she was talking now to all the Star Colonels as well as the Galaxy Commander. "Small World! Of what use to us is a place whose very *name* proclaims its insignificance?"

"If the Star Colonel had ever planned a long-term campaign, instead of fighting in the campaigns of others," Radick said, "she would perhaps understand the need for incorporating more worlds into our power base."

Anastasia sneered. "We are Wolves; we are our own power base. And what will the rulers of the Inner Sphere say of us when they look at this campaign?"

She paused and let the silence drag out, waiting for the intake of breath and slight shift in expression that told her Radick was about to speak. Then she spoke first, forestalling him: "I will tell you what they will say. They will say, 'The Steel Wolves are no real threat to us. They choose easy targets these days because their leader, Kal Radick, is a cautious man.' "

There, she thought. I have said it. He will hear the word: *Coward*.

She saw the ugly flare of anger in his eyes before he suppressed it, and knew that she had him. She pushed on.

"I say again, Galaxy Commander, I am bidding myself against you in a Trial of Possession, your rank and position to be the stakes. Augmented or unaugmented, your choice."

Radick looked down at her, letting their position emphasize his extra inches of height. "Unaugmented, Star Colonel. Name a time and a place where we can come together, and let this meeting return to its scheduled business."

"The time is now, and the place is here." She turned to Star Colonel Marks, who happened to be the nearest of the assembled Warriors. "Clear the floor and make a ring. The Galaxy Commander and I are going to fight."

18

Steel Wolf Headquarters
The Four Cities, Tigress
May, 3133; local summer

Anastasia stood a little way away from Kal Radick as the chairs were moved and stacked, and the big map table, its tri-vee display extinguished, was shoved up against the room's far back wall. Once the floor was cleared, the senior officers present formed the ring. The other officers and MechWarriors crowded close behind them as eager spectators—some even climbed up onto the table for a better view. There were more people present than Anastasia remembered; word of the proposed Trial must have spread while she and Kal Radick were talking.

The last chair was moved, and the circle closed. Without bothering to see if Radick followed, Anastasia stepped inside.

She heard his footstep on the tile floor behind

her. He had not hesitated. Once she had reached the center of the circle, she turned to face him. He was standing closer to her than she had thought, and he was smiling.

He pulled off his uniform tunic and tossed it aside, out of the ring. He moved with a carelessness that implied contempt for his opponent, as if he didn't care whether she attacked or not. Any assault would be brushed aside.

"So, Anastasia," he said. "You look thoughtful. Are you not so eager to fight me, after all?"

"As eager as you are," Anastasia said. "And more."

She knew that Radick's careless pose was a deliberate misdirection. She could see how his feet were planted, how he was keeping his center of gravity low, how he was making sure that she stayed inside his field of view—the forward hundred twenty degrees that defined human eyesight.

Anastasia took a step forward. Her own mass was centered and her breathing was steady and slow. "Are you ready?"

"I am," Radick said. "If you win, my rank and position are yours. If you lose—would you prefer that I kill you, or let you live? If I leave your face unmarked, you may be able to work your way home to Arc-Royal on your back."

She had been expecting a deliberate insult, an attempt to throw her mind and emotions off balance before the start of battle, and Radick's choice of slurs was as unimaginative as she had suspected it would be. She set aside the anger that rose up in her just the same, and let it fade from her consciousness like everything else in the room except the circle in which she stood.

"You are all talk, Kal Radick," she said, and deliberately turned her back on the Galaxy Commander.

In the same moment that she turned, she began a subvocal count. And one and two and—

She leapt up, spinning, and felt, as she had expected, the breeze of a blow aimed at her back, a punch at full extension that might have snapped her spine. It struck only empty air.

Anastasia landed on her feet behind and to one side of Kal Radick, and continued her spin without pause. She brought her right leg up and forward, driving a snap-kick into his back on the level of his left kidney. Radick staggered forward, but kept his footing.

Damn, she thought. That kick came in too light.

Radick had already been moving forward in the same direction as her strike. Now he was touched—hurt, perhaps—but not crippled.

"Very—good," he gasped.

He turned, pivoting on the balls of his feet, then lowered his hands and made a grab for the heel of Anastasia's still-raised foot. Catching it, he pulled backward and up. Anastasia lost her balance and fell.

She let herself go with the fall, tucking into a roll instead of landing on her back with stunning force, and came up on her feet and in guard position: feet wide, knees flexed, hands palm up at waist height.

"And you are not good enough," she said. "Not to command the Wolves."

Radick did not answer—not with words. He turned sideways to her and brought up his left foot to knee level, and she prepared herself to meet an incoming side kick. Instead, he leapt and lunged, his right hand aimed like a spear at her solar plexus. A hard enough blow there, in the nerve bundle below her breastbone, and nothing else would matter. Her own body would betray her.

An outside block with her right hand turned the blow. But Radick must have anticipated that defense, because her hand touched only air, and in the next fractional instant Radick's left hand punched in hard on her biceps, sending an electric wave of pain down to the tips of her fingers.

A gasp—of surprise? of admiration?—came from one of the spectators, somewhere outside the ring. Kal Radick had known what his opponent would do, and had aimed to strike her muscle while it was contracted and at its most vulnerable. Anastasia's right hand would be useless for a while, and if Radick had ruptured the muscle her whole arm would be useless for the rest of the fight and for some time thereafter.

Anastasia reacted without thinking. Her left hand swept up and in, and she struck down onto Radick's collarbone with the knife-edge of the hand. She felt two bones break under the impact—the medial carpal bone in her own left hand, and Kal Radick's clavicle. Now each of them was down an arm—with his broken collarbone, Radick's left hand hung as useless as Anastasia's right arm.

"We shall see who commands the Wolves," Radick said.

He raised his right knee as if trying to jab it into her belly, then snapped forward with his foot. The vicious kick might have crippled her if it had struck her kneecap, where it had been clearly aimed.

Anastasia didn't waste breath. Instead she kicked out at the left leg that supported her opponent in his attack. He turned to slip the blow, and Anastasia sprang forward, throwing the whole weight of her body against him. The two of them went down in a tangle together: Kal Radick on the bottom; Anastasia above him and facing away.

So far so good, but in a prolonged fight, the larger and more muscular Radick would have an advantage in stamina. She had to end the combat now if she didn't want to lose.

Anastasia jabbed her left elbow backward at full strength into Kal Radick's torso, and struck meat. She pulled her arm forward and struck back again at the same point. This time she was rewarded with the sound of a sharp exhalation, and a solid impact that told her she was hitting Radick's rib cage.

But Radick still had not given up. He threw an arm around Anastasia's neck and pulled backward, cutting into her windpipe and choking off the blood in the arteries that fed her brain, and not letting go. Blackness gathered at the edges of her vision. If she let the blackness take her, the night would never leave her and she would die.

She struck again with her elbow. The solid ribs that she struck cracked. Another blow in the same place—she could no longer feel her elbow; had she dislocated it?—and the ribs became suddenly softer. Again and again she struck, feeling the ribs fragmenting beneath her blows while her lungs cried out for air and the blackness rose steadily behind her eyes.

At length she felt Radick's arm fall from around her neck. She rolled away from him, and without the aid of either arm—both of them were useless now—she staggered to her feet and looked down at where Kal Radick lay choking and struggling for breath. The Galaxy Commander's face had gone gray and was covered with sweat, and pink-tinged foam bubbled from his lips and nose.

"Punctured a lung, did I?" Anastasia said. The blackness had receded from her vision, leaving an array of floating bright spots in its place. "No worry. I can fix it."

She dropped full weight with both knees onto Radick's chest. More of his ribs snapped as he convulsed under the blow. She struggled back to her feet and dropped kneeling onto his chest for a second time. This time he didn't move, and it felt like dropping onto a sack of wet sand.

Still kneeling on Kal Radick's lifeless chest, Anastasia looked up at the ring of spectators. "This Trial is over," she said.

Her voice was scarcely more than a harsh rasp, and she drew each breath with difficulty—her throat had begun swelling from the damage that it had sustained when Radick had gotten his forearm across her neck and pulled back. But there was no other sound in the room except her words.

"I am the Galaxy Commander now. I, Anastasia—"

"Kerensky!" shouted a voice from outside the ring. Then again, in chorus, "Kerensky!" out of many throats.

"Yes," Anastasia said. "We have been quiet too long, my Wolves. But soon all the worlds—soon Terra herself—will hear us howl."

She stood. She did not allow herself to sway, in spite of the fact that the room was spinning around her. She walked forward, out of the ring.

"I am going to my quarters," she said. "Star Colonels, tonight, report to me. Be prepared to tell me how soon you will be ready for combat operations. Our target is no longer Small World. It is Northwind."

19

Clan DropShip **Lupus**
Northwind Drop Point
Prefecture III, Republic of the Sphere
June, 3133; no season

"Immediately," when speaking of a full-scale invasion of Northwind, still required a certain amount of time spent in preparation, even for a Steel Wolf force already bent on attacking Small World. By the time the Wolves left Tigress, Anastasia Kerensky's bruises from her fight with Kal Radick were fading, although her hand was still splinted. The injury was not important—she had no need for those fingers in either planning strategy or riding a 'Mech—so she ignored it.

During her time aboard the DropShip *Lupus,* she made a point of seeking out and talking with as many different elements of the Steel Wolf invasion force as possible—seeing and being seen, letting people know directly that the new Galaxy Commander was not at all the same as the old one. The get-acquainted process also gave her a better feel for the strength and composition of the force for this mission than she could get from cold words and numbers on a notepad or in a file. There were other Steel Wolf resources in the Prefecture engaged in other missions. She'd worry about them another time.

The news for now was both bad and good. On the bad side, the Wolves—like everybody else these days, it seemed—had more qualified MechWarriors than proper 'Mechs to carry them into battle. The invasion force possessed a *Koshi*, a *MadCat*, and a *Catapult*, plus her own *Ryoken II;* beyond that, the MechWarriors had to make do with retrofitted Industrial and Forestry-Mechs. Thinking about it, she could not resist an inward sneer. The Wolves should never have given up their BattleMechs, no matter what Devlin Stone had promised them in return.

On the good side, the Steel Wolves had more than a sufficiency of tanks and other vehicles, both troop transports and motorized cavalry. Another pleasant surprise, this one on a more personal level, came from her perusal of the personnel files: Nicholas Darwin had turned out to possess an excellent battlefield record, as well as the respect of his peers among the tank officers.

She could use that. If she decided to promote him—as she was toying with the idea of doing—she would have at least one Star Colonel firmly on her side in the coming fight. Which would mean a smaller chance of accidental or deliberate sabotage of her plans, and a better chance of actually having them understood.

She could have used more air and aerospace craft; Radick and his chosen commanders had spent those elements heavily in the past few campaigns. As matters stood, the Steel Wolves had sufficient helicopters and VTOL craft for close air support, and enough aerospace fighters to either take out the air defenses over Tara or protect their DropShips from aerial assault after landing, but not enough to do a full-scale job of both.

The Steel Wolves also had units of both regular and Elemental infantry—though again, not nearly as much of the latter as she would have liked. Still, the invasion force overall was fairly heavy on infantry, and she would have to craft her battle plan to make use of it. The mix was not exactly as she would have liked, but it was adequate, and she would play the hand that she had been given.

Anastasia looked at the maps of Northwind, and at the data in the Galaxy Commander's files, and pondered strategy. The character of the opposing commander was always an important consideration, and the news in that department was both good and bad. Kal Radick's most recent intelligence reports put Prefect Tara Campbell in residence on Northwind, backed up by a Paladin of the Sphere. Northwind was Tara Campbell's home world, and she was its Countess, which gave her strong ties to the place, plus strong loyalty from the local forces. Add to that a Paladin's authority and resources and the corresponding boost to morale in general . . . and the combination could mean trouble.

On the other hand, a divided command held considerable potential for disputes in authority. The Paladin technically outranked the Prefect, and could overrule her decisions if he so chose. If the two of them had not managed to achieve a working partnership, they would be fighting each other as much as the enemy, and both efficiency and morale would suffer.

Anastasia Kerensky contemplated that possibility, and felt a certain amount of justified scorn. Among the Clans, such a situation would never be allowed the chance to develop. There would be a Trial, and the question would be settled. One way or the other.

The Prefect herself remained something of an unknown quantity. Her public record was open, true . . . but a public record showed only the surface of a person's words and actions, not the reasons or motivations beneath. Tara Campbell's exchange of hot words with Kal Radick, for example, in the days before the HPG net fell apart—her remarks could have been either a calculated insult or an accidental one, depending upon whether the Prefect was recklessly aggressive or merely quick-tempered and somewhat naive.

Not, Anastasia thought with a smile, that either alternative argued well for the Countess being a strategic thinker of any great ability. The Paladin, on the other hand, was almost guaranteed to be a proven Warrior and Commander.

Once again, much depended on how well Prefect and Paladin could work together.

Anastasia knew better than to count on incompetence and dissension. She would assume that Tara Campbell and her Paladin had achieved some kind of understanding, and would formulate her plans accordingly.

Twenty-four hours before the DropShips made contact with Northwind, she called a meeting of her senior commanders in *Lupus*'s tactical room. When they arrived, she had a map of Northwind lit up and tagged on the display table: the large continent of New Lanark; the second landmass, almost as large, that was oil- and mineral-rich Kearny; and Halidon, the third and smallest of the three continents.

She tapped on the table to draw the officers' attention. "Take a good look," she told them. "This is what we are going after."

Her Star Colonels gathered around the table. She was a bit surprised to see that Nicholas Darwin was among them, although neither she nor he changed expressions or allowed themselves to betray any reaction. They had not had the opportunity to share a conversation, or a bed, since the invasion force had boarded the DropShips. She presumed that Darwin had been bunking with the other tank officers, while she herself, as befit a Galaxy Commander, slept in the isolated splendor of private quarters.

His appearance now as a Star Colonel somewhat startled her. She had not known that there had been a Trial of Position during the voyage. The affair would have been routine, then. Nothing out of the ordinary had taken place to make it worth the Galaxy Commander's attention.

She set the new development aside for later consideration—once the fighting on Northwind was done, she would have to congratulate Nicholas properly—and continued her talk.

"Here is our overall strategy. If need be, we can change and adapt it to fresh information and changed conditions, but the basic outline is here. Northwind has two DropPorts, one here, near the capital city of Tara"—she indicated a flashing red light on the largest landmass—"and one small port here, on Halidon"—she indicated a second flashing light. "The DropPort for the city of Tara is heavily defended, because it is the place where they expect ships to land."

She looked around at her assembled commanders and grinned. "So we will not be landing at the main port. The Halidon DropPort would be the obvious second choice. But it is isolated, and a long way from our main targets. Also, it has a resident aerospace training contingent, and while I doubt the cadets there would count as serious opponents, they could make taking the Halidon DropPort harder than its size is worth.

"So. We bypass the working DropPorts entirely. But here"—she indicated a large blank area on the main continental mass—"on the interior plains of New Lanark, on the opposite side of the Rockspire Mountains from the capital"—a touch of a button, and the mountain range that formed the spine of the continent lit up in shades of green—"are natural salt flats that served in the early days of Northwind's settlement as the functional equivalent of a DropPort landing field. We will take the DropShips down there. Our aerospace contingent will be taking out the electronic orbital spy satellites, dealing with the aerospace fighters over Tara, and keeping the Highlanders busy on the other side of the mountains.

"Meanwhile, our forces pass through the Rockspires at this point." She indicated a winding line in red passing through the green of the mountains. "The locals call it Red Ledge Pass. As you can see, it leads through the mountains and out onto the open plains just north of the capital. Once through the Rockspires, we are within a day's striking range of Tara.

"And once we have Tara," she concluded, "we have Northwind."

PART THREE

Northwind, Late Spring 3133
Standing Guard

20

Castle Northwind
Northwind
April, 3133; local spring

Castle Northwind, official residence of the Counts and Countesses of Northwind, was a big gray stone pseudo-Gothic pile, built by one of the early Northwind Campbells out of nostalgia for similar buildings back on Terra. Unlike its architectural predecessors, this latter-day version wasn't actually a defensible fortress; Northwind had never gone through a swords-and-armor feudal age that would have required one.

Nevertheless, the castle was an impressive structure, high-walled and many-towered, situated on a green hill above a deep spring-fed highland lake. Banners snapped in the wind that blew across its battlements, and all around the valley that held it rose the gray, glacier-scarred peaks of the northern Rockspires.

The Countess of Northwind and Paladin Ezekiel Crow were at work in the castle solar, a large, airy room at the top of the main tower. Afternoon sunlight streamed in through the leaded-glass panes of the tall windows, illuminating the remains of a working lunch spread out on the central table. The crumbled leftovers of a beef roast wrapped in pastry shared space with file folders and data pads and other administrative debris.

"Didn't I tell you that we'd get a lot more done if we did our work here instead of in the city?" Tara Campbell said.

"We've had fewer interruptions while we've been working here, at any rate," Crow admitted.

"That's because there isn't any place in the city where I'm not on the job and available to anyone who needs to see me," she said. "When I come back to Castle Northwind, I'm at home, and the staff here has known me so long that they're almost family. They know better than to let people bother me if I don't want to be bothered."

"I suppose it's one of the advantages to growing up in a castle." He smiled briefly. "Like a princess in one of the old stories."

"Happily ever after . . . at least until my mother died. Then my father went back to military service, and after that we lived here, there, and everywhere." She paused a moment to pick up the loose papers on the table and stack them neatly. "Where did you grow up?"

"Liao."

She looked at him, reminded again that he

was older than he appeared. "Oh. Were you there during—"

His expression, always reserved, closed off even more. "During the Massacre? Yes."

She felt a surge of embarrassment at her own verbal clumsiness. "I'm sorry. I didn't mean to bring up painful memories."

Everybody in The Republic of the Sphere knew the story, after all: how agents of the Capellan Confederation fomented unrest on Liao, making it into a perpetual thorn in the side for The Republic of the Sphere; how a traitor working at Liao's DropPort had allowed an unauthorized CapCon ship to land; how the streets of Chang-an had run red with blood before the CapCons were done with Liao and The Republic of the Sphere was done with them.

"It's all right," he said. "It happened a long time ago. It's just painful still, sometimes. Both my parents died in the city fighting, during the early days."

"You were close to your parents?"

"Not close enough, as it turned out," he said. "I couldn't get home in time to save them."

"I can't imagine. . . ." On impulse, she laid her hand lightly on his arm for a moment before taking it away, and felt his muscles go tense under even that briefest of touches. "My parents are gone, too. Nothing as bad as—as what happened on Liao. But I still miss them."

The moment was interrupted by a rumbling in the air and a rattling of the glass in the windows. A shadow passed across the clipped green lawn outside.

Ezekiel Crow froze, listening, then relaxed. "VTOL craft going over."

"Coming down, more likely," she said. "We're not on any regular flight paths, and—unfortunately for our continued lack of interruptions—Headquarters knows that I'm here."

"I don't hear it landing."

"There are a couple of densely wooded hills between here and the VTOL pad and that cuts down on the noise pollution and preserves the view." She pressed the housekeeper's call button set into the wall by the door. "Mrs. Danvers? Put some tea and some hearty sandwiches on hot standby. I think we're going to have visitors."

Their visitor, a quarter-hour later, turned out to be Colonel Michael Griffin. By the time the Colonel arrived in the solar, all evidence of the earlier working lunch had been cleared away and replaced by a porcelain tea service and a platter of sliced bread, meat, and cheese. Griffin filled his plate with the polite concentration of a man who had already missed lunch and was anticipating missing dinner.

"What brings you here in such haste, Colonel?" Tara asked.

"Strategic consultation," he said. "That's something best done face-to-face. There's no telling who's keeping an ear on electronic transmissions these days."

Ezekiel Crow looked at him darkly. "Are you suggesting to the Countess that there might be traitors on Northwind?"

Colonel Griffin paused and gave Crow a level glance over the top edge of his tea cup. "I work in intelligence, my lord. Assuming traitors is part of my job."

Tara, listening, suppressed a sigh. The two of them were doing it again, bristling up at each other like dogs; she wondered if they even realized she noticed.

As if I didn't have enough work to do, she thought, without the two people I most depend on pushing and sniping at each other every time they're together in the same room. That was one of the reasons I brought Crow to Castle Northwind to work in the first place, to get him out of Griffin's way.

Oil on troubled waters time, Tara, she told herself. It's all part of the job.

"It doesn't even need a traitor to mess things up," she said. "Just somebody on-planet with different loyalties or a different agenda. And even with the HPG network down, we still get enough travelers for there to be plenty of those."

Griffin looked somewhat mollified. "It keeps me busy, I can tell you." He sipped at his tea. "Today's a case in point."

"How's that?" she asked.

"We've got a DropShip in at the port, and it's brought along the usual pile of mail and newsdiscs." The Colonel opened the leather valise he'd brought with him and took out a disc. "Including this one from General Davies on Quentin. Is there a player in here?"

Tara nodded at the polished wood tri-vee cabinet set against the far wall next to the call button. "In there."

Griffin opened the cabinet and put the disc into the player. The tri-vee filled with images of Quentin, fading into and replacing one another—the DropShip landing field; a ship descending, the image cut off suddenly in a blaze of light; a *Tundra Wolf* BattleMech, seen in jerky, narrow-field motion from inside a fast-moving vehicle; armored infantry, firing Gauss rifles at something outside of the image. Ship and 'Mech and infantry armor all bore Steel Wolf insignia.

The images continued, now with a voiceover running along with them.

"General Gwyn Davies, Commander of the Highlander forces on Quentin, speaking. Two weeks ago, Quentin came under attack by elements of the Steel Wolf faction under the command of Star Colonel Ulan. Their apparent target was the industrial district in Port Frome, since factories there produce the necessary elements for conversion of Agricultural and ForestryMechs into battleworthy configurations. It is my pleasure at this time to report that the Wolves were repulsed after sharp fighting; the rest of this disc contains full intelligence summaries and battle data on the conflict."

The end of the brief speech coincided with the cube display's final image: Steel Wolf DropShips rising from the landing field, and fadeout. The image loop started to repeat, Colonel Griffin hit the stop button, and Crow and Tara and Griffin looked at one another.

"Well," said Tara, after a long silence. "We've been wondering for months exactly who we were going to have to fight. I think that now we know."

21

Castle Northwind
Northwind
April, 3133; local spring

Several hours after Colonel Michael Griffin had departed from Castle Northwind, Tara Campbell and Ezekiel Crow remained at work in the solar chamber, burning the midnight oil—or at least, the midnight electrons. Clouds had darkened the skies over the castle as the afternoon drew on toward sunset, and nightfall brought with it a fast-moving spring storm. Thunder rumbled outside the windows, and strong gusts of wind dashed heavy raindrops against the leaded-glass panes. Flashes of lightning illuminated the dark, lowering clouds and the wind-tossed trees on the mountain slopes beneath.

Tara waved a hand at the weather outside. "I

used to love watching bad weather from this room when I was a little girl."

Another flash of lightning lit up the turbulent waters of the lake below the castle.

"It's certainly dramatic," Ezekiel Crow acknowledged.

"I always liked how solid the castle felt, no matter what was going on outside." She laughed. "Then I got older, and found out that the weather we have around here is nothing. Down by Tara—the city, I mean; do you have any idea how annoyed I still am at my parents, sometimes?—the summer storms can tear down buildings."

"Not good weather to fight in, to be sure."

She sighed, and turned back to the papers and display pads on the table. "I know. But unless Radick and the Steel Wolves exercise a lot more patience than intelligence reports give them credit for, we're probably going to have to."

Ezekiel Crow picked up a data pad with the latest manpower reports. "At least the on-planet elements of the Regiments are coming up to full strength. That was a good thought, to start the recruitment drives."

"Thanks." She could feel herself blushing, and turned her head away to hide it—that was the curse of a fair skin, that every passing change of color showed up like neon. "When Katana Tormark left, I was afraid I was going to drop the ball completely, because I knew how unprepared I was for this job. All I could do was keep my chin up and hope that nobody else noticed how scared I was."

Ezekiel Crow gave her a curious look. "It never occurred to you to decline the promotion?"

"If I'd thought that there was anybody else available with the right combination of family and training—then, trust me, I would have turned this job down in a heartbeat. But there wasn't."

"So it was a matter of doing your duty to The Republic?"

"Something like that, yes," she said. "I know it sounds sentimental, but—"

"There's nothing wrong with feeling a sentimental attachment to one's home. But it's unusual to find someone thinking about The Republic of the Sphere in that fashion."

"It *shouldn't* be unusual, though," she said. "Making it not be unusual was what Devlin Stone was trying to do in the first place. Encouraging immigration, breaking up the factions—"

"Which didn't work, unfortunately." Crow looked grim now. "Duchess Tormark is an excellent example."

Tara felt the sudden surge of an old anger. "If Duchess Tormark had kept faith with The Republic like she ought to have done, then the Dragon's Fury would still be just a bunch of disaffected misfits instead of a serious military threat."

"One could say the same thing of Galaxy Commander Kal Radick. Who is, face it, a much more immediate threat than the Dragon's Fury."

"I suppose so." Tara exhaled and drew a calming breath. "But I never expected anything better of Radick or the Clans. They're not assimilated, no matter how much they pretend to be. Katana, though . . . we had the same training, we swore the same oaths . . . and she threw it away, she made it all into *nothing*."

"A betrayal."

"Yes."

Crow gazed out at the darkness beyond the rain-slashed windows, his expression distant and thoughtful. "It's always possible that she sees things differently."

"So that's all treason is—a case of different people seeing things differently?"

"That's one way to look at it."

The anger she felt at Katana Tormark's defection was still with her, making her voice sharper than she intended. "I suppose it was someone 'seeing things differently' who let the CapCons put down that DropShip on Liao."

He went very still, almost as if she'd slapped him, and spoke carefully and distantly. "Nobody knows why it was done."

"I'm sorry," she said. "I didn't mean to—"

"The betrayer of Liao was never found. So many people died—he would have been just one more body, buried in a common grave like all the others."

She swallowed, feeling sick. "Your parents, too?"

"Yes."

"I *am* sorry."

He drew a deep breath and visibly put the memories behind him. "It was a long time ago. But I haven't forgotten. It's one of the reasons I chose the career that I did, and why I worked so hard to reach the place where I am now. I don't want anything like that to ever happen again."

22

Tyson and Varney 'Mech Factory
Fairfield, Northwind
May, 3133; local spring

Tyson and Varney, Limited, had built most of the Mining- and ConstructionMechs currently in use on Northwind, and held the contracts for most of the unbuilt ones. Since the winter of 3132, Tyson and Varney had also held the Northwind Highlanders' contract for retrofitting work 'Mechs to combat models.

Today Colonel Michael Griffin had come to Fairfield in order to pay an official visit on Tyson and Varney's main plant. Griffin, who had made no secret of the fact that he was there to check on the company's progress, was escorted around the factory by the senior plant manager, a stocky, thick-mustached individual named Evans.

The plant was a series of immense assembly

hangars, each subdivided into three or four bays. Each bay held a 'Mech in progress, worked on by teams of a dozen or more men and women under the glare of sodium vapor lights. Hoarse voices shouted back and forth, metal clanged and crashed and groaned against metal, and the 'Mech bays were full of the hiss and spark of welding torches and the smell of ozone.

The workers in their safety goggles and heavy protective earmuffs looked like strange, bulbous-headed insects crawling over the giant anthropomorphic shapes of the 'Mechs. Colonel Griffin, encountering the noise and the dazzle of the 'Mech bays for the first time, felt grateful for the pair of yellow foam plugs that Evans had insisted he put into his ears before entering the hangar.

The manager waved an arm in the direction of the 'Mechs in the first three bays.

"These are the farthest along," he said, shouting to make himself heard over the din. "They're out-of-the-box models, no custom mods, so retrofitting them to your specs doesn't mean ripping anything else out first."

Griffin followed the manager's gesture and looked at the nearest 'Mech. He wished he knew enough about design and engineering to estimate the workers' rate of progress. "How soon until these are finished?"

"This lot? About a month. The ForestryMechs in the next bays over, maybe a week after that."

Griffin suppressed his sinking feeling with difficulty. "No faster?"

"We're not just stamping out stuff with cookie cutters here," Evans said, scowling. "There's a lot more one-of-a-kind handiwork goes into making these babies than most people think, and retrofitting them into units that can fight is a lot trickier than it looks."

"I'm sure it is," Griffin said hastily. "How about the new construction?"

"I won't lie to you. It's going a lot slower than we'd like."

"The Prefect isn't going to be very happy about that."

"The Prefect will just have to live with it," the manager said. "It turns out that designing a reconfigured IndustrialMech or ForestryMech from the ground up is only a couple of notches short of designing a full-scale BattleMech, and that's a tough job. Not that Tyson and Varney couldn't handle it, if you gave us all the right materials."

"I'm certain you could," said Griffin. "But what you're telling me right now is that the new construction isn't going to be coming on-line any time in the immediate future."

"I don't like being the bearer of bad news . . . but yeah, that's about it. We can slap the design engineers around a bit, remind them they're not supposed to be inventing the next generation in BattleMech technology here, but it's still not going to change any of the basic problems."

For a moment, Griffin considered ordering the shutdown of the redesign project. His mandate from Tara Campbell extended as far as that, he thought, even if his nominal authority didn't;

and if he stated for the record that he thought the 'Mech redesign program was a failure and ought to be closed down, the Countess would probably back his decision.

Griffin remained in silent thought long enough to notice the manager sweating. Finally he said, "Keep that part of the project going anyway. It may not be of much help to us in the short term, but in the long term . . . in the long term, Mr. Evans, I'm very much afraid that things are going to be different. And your design engineers may yet get their wish."

"I'll tell them what you said," the manager told him, and Griffin could see the man's relief, somewhat tempered by his understanding of what Griffin had implied for the future. "Right now, I believe that if we reallocate resources and manpower and go to round-the-clock shifts, we can have the first retrofitted units ready to roll in three weeks or a bit less."

"That would be good," Griffin said. "I'll make certain that the Prefect has your estimate."

The manager gave him a gloomy look. "Which had better be binding, I suppose."

Griffin smiled. "You said it, Mr. Evans. I didn't."

23

The New Barracks
Tara, Northwind
June, 3133; local summer

Tara Campbell was asleep in the Prefect's quarters in the New Barracks when the wall speaker buzzed. She came fully awake in an instant when a voice began speaking immediately without waiting for an acknowledgment—an override at this hour never meant good news.

"Prefect Campbell, please come to the Combat Information Center."

Another buzz from the speaker, and the voice repeated, "Prefect Campbell, please come to the Combat Information Center."

Tara was already out of bed and scrambling for her clothes. "On my way."

She dressed in haste: plain working uniform, first item in the closet and the easiest to grab; enough underwear to be decent; hair finger combed and cleared back from her face with a stretch knit band. She was halfway to the Fort and the CIC before she realized that she was wearing not regulation shoes and socks, but her favorite pair of ancient bedroom slippers.

The hell with it, she thought. Northwind could survive the knowledge that its Countess wore fleece-lined tartan moccasins.

She wouldn't be the only person who'd gotten an unexpected wake-up call, either. The courtyards and corridors of the Fort were full of people in uniform heading places with purposeful speed. Alarms clamored in the halls and stairwells as she made her way down to the bombproof chamber in the depths of the Fort that housed the Combat Information Center for Northwind's local defense forces.

When she reached her destination, Colonel Michael Griffin, whose quarters were closer to CIC than hers, was already there, pacing back and forth amid the uniformed specialists who monitored the display screens on CIC's array of communications and data consoles. Ezekiel Crow had VIP housing in a distant wing of the Fort complex; he arrived at a run forty-five seconds after Tara. The Paladin's normally flawless uniform tunic and trousers looked tired and wrinkled. Tara could only guess that the nearest complete set to hand when the summons came had been the ones he'd taken off the evening before.

"What's the word?" Tara asked Griffin as soon as she'd caught her breath.

"Steel Wolf DropShips have entered the system," the Colonel said. "They've been taking out our surveillance and weapons platforms as they go. The Far Point observation post reported their presence and then went dead."

"Good on Far Point for getting the message through," said Tara.

That brief accolade was all that she could afford to give the station and its people at the moment. If they weren't dead already, they had a decent chance of being alive to collect their combat pay when the fighting was over. It all depended on whether the Wolves had simply fried the station's comms and sensors in passing, or taken the time to blow the whole post to hell and gone.

"The Wolves don't want us tracking them," Ezekiel Crow said. His features were set and grim; Tara wondered if he was remembering what had happened after the Capellan Confederation descended on Liao. "They want to make us guess where they're coming down."

"Then we'll just have to be ready to jump in any direction," Tara said. "And make certain our ground-based comms stay good."

Colonel Griffin frowned. "I don't like this. All our current intel on the Steel Wolves says Kal Radick is more straightforward than that."

"Maybe there's been a change of command," Ezekiel Crow suggested. "It's not inconceivable that the Wolves could have produced somebody with enough nerve to challenge Radick for his position, as well as enough of whatever else it takes to beat him."

Tara filled a mug with strong black tea from CIC's galley urn and added milk and sugar, using the time to think about what had been said. The Paladin and Colonel Griffin, though less mutually antagonistic than they had been initially, were never going to be the best of friends, and any issue upon which they were in agreement demanded serious consideration. "As of the last DropShip to come in with news from Tigress, Radick was still the man in charge."

Griffin said, "The ship hit three other worlds in between leaving Tigress and coming here. That's plenty of time for news to go stale."

"Assume that the leader is still Radick, then," Tara said. "But draw up contingency plans in case it's somebody else."

Colonel Griffin nodded. "We have intelligence files on most of his prominent or rising subordinate officers. But if Radick's been supplanted, I think our analysts need to put in a requisition chit for a better grade of crystal ball, because nobody on the list was tagged as a serious threat to the Galaxy Commander's position."

"People change," Tara said. "Maybe somebody on Radick's staff woke up feeling ambitious one morning and never bothered to let us know."

Ezekiel Crow looked grave. "Perhaps. Or perhaps this hypothetical person is a wild card in the game, one for whom we have no helpful profiles or contingency plans. We must ready ourselves to deal with the unexpected."

"Meanwhile," said Tara, "we can start mobilizing the defense forces. And wait to see where to send them."

24

Regimental Base near Tara
Northwind
June, 3133; local summer

"Up, up, up!"

The lights snapped on. Will Elliot, thrown out of a sound sleep by the shouted orders and by the strident clamor of the alarm, put up an arm to shield his eyes from the sudden glare. In the same movement he rolled out of his bunk—he knew better by now than to question a Sergeant's voice.

"Move it, people!" the Sergeant was shouting. The barracks began to fill with the sound of lockers banging open and shut. "On your feet, on the grinder, full kit, combat loadout. Five minutes. We're burning time, people."

Will unlocked and raised the base of his bunk. His uniform lay inside. He snapped it on quickly, then pulled on his socks and boots. On impulse, he stuffed an extra pair of clean, dry socks into his outermost pocket. A visible bulge like that would never pass inspection, but Will didn't think he needed to worry about passing inspection right now.

He closed his locker and left the bunkroom. Once out in the corridor, he joined a stream of other soldiers heading down the passageway to the left, where the armory door stood open. The tight press of so many individuals all heading in the same direction with single-minded intent reminded him of a raft of migratory eels running upstream at spawning time. Eels died when they reached the spawning-beds . . . maybe that wasn't such a good thing to be thinking about right now, after all.

Inside the armory, the Gauss rifles waited in their racks.

"Elliot, William A.," Will said to the armorer as he came up. "Four-nine-one-zero-seven."

"Here's your weapon, Elliot," the armorer said. "Down the passage, draw your charge and your spares."

"Don't you want me to sign—"

"No, move it. Next! Pick it up, people!"

Will took his Gauss rifle and held it at trail arms as he walked quickly down the passageway. He didn't know yet what was happening, but he had a feeling it was serious. This was the first time he hadn't been required first to sign for his rifle and then inspect it under the armorer's gaze.

Ahead of him, boxes stacked on one side of the corridor were filled with the metal slugs fired by the infantry's Thunderstroke Gauss rifles. A Sergeant stood by the open crates.

"Pick up your load. Keep moving," the Sergeant said.

Will grabbed up the slugs and power packs and stuffed them into the pockets of his battle fatigues. He was halfway down the steps to the parade ground before he realized that he'd automatically stowed the material in the standard pockets and the standard configurations that had been drilled into him in boot camp. Now he understood the reason for that drill, and for how it had been reinforced at the time by the voices of Sergeants in his ears and by the push-ups meted out for the smallest deviation from the standard.

He was trotting, no hint of weariness now, despite the hour. Even in boot camp, everyone had known that sooner or later there was going to be trouble—where from, though, was another question, and one that recruits weren't expected to have an answer to.

Probably because nobody else had an answer, either, Will thought as he found his place on the paved strip where the scout/sniper platoon mustered. But it looked like they were going to get one now.

Jock Gordon was already there on the strip, a big man standing easy. He was the youngest son from a farm family in the grain and dairy country to the northeast, and had joined the Regiment because he'd grown bored with working on land that was already divided up among his three older brothers.

Will took position beside Jock. A moment later Lexa McIntosh fell in beside them.

"What's the word?" Lexa asked. She was a hell-raiser from the Kearny outback, gypsy-dark and barely tall enough to make the recruiters' minimum, but a dead shot with any weapon she could lift high enough to aim. As one of the unit's expert marksmen, she carried a Starfire ER laser rifle instead of a Thunderstroke Gauss.

"You know as much as I do," Jock said back. "One minute there I am, dreaming of home and the love of a good woman—"

"And I'm not good enough? I like that, I do."

"—a good woman who won't come after me with a combat knife the first time she thinks I'm looking at someone else, and the next moment I'm out the door with a pack on my back and a rifle in my hand."

Their questions were answered a moment later. A Sergeant climbed to the top of a truck and shouted, "Company, ten-SHUN!"

Instantly, the Highlanders stopped talking and snapped to attention.

"Listen up," the Sergeant said. "Here's what I know. About two hours ago the Steel Wolves brought their DropShips into the Northwind system. Now, maybe the Wolves came here to drink tea and have a friendly chat, but if they didn't, then we're going to kick their sorry asses off our planet. By squads, mount up. We're moving out."

He pointed to the truck at the head of the column behind him. "First company, Platoon A, squads one, two, and three get in truck one. Make sure your safeties are on. Go, go, go."

He continued down the list, naming the squads and packing them into the trucks. As each truck filled, it pulled away and started down the road.

"And to think that I joined up because the judge said 'Three years with the Regiment, girl, or four in jail,' " Lexa said. "If I'd had any sense, I'd have told him, 'jail,' and still be asleep in my bed tonight."

"If the Steel Wolves are coming, jail won't be any safer," Will replied. "At least this way you'll get to fight back."

Then their unit was called: "Scout/snipers, Unit Four, mount up. Move it, people. We don't have all day."

"Nor all night, either," Jock Gordon said as he swung himself over the side of the truck, the last of their platoon to climb aboard. His words were covered by the sound of heavy engines moving from an idle to a roaring full power. The truck lurched, and they were on their way.

Will looked at his watch. Less than a quarter hour ago, he'd been asleep. Now he was on his way to war.

25

The Fort
City of Tara, Northwind
June, 3133; local summer

"The DropShips are down."

Tara Campbell knew that she must have slept at least occasionally during the almost two weeks it had taken for the Steel Wolves to make it from the jump point to Northwind's planetary surface. She wasn't wearing the tartan bedroom slippers anymore, for one thing, although she couldn't remember either going back to her quarters or changing uniforms. What rest she'd gotten, however, hadn't come often enough or lasted long enough to keep the weariness out of her voice.

She didn't even want to contemplate what she looked like. Michael Griffin and Ezekiel Crow hadn't gotten any more sleep than she had, and in the dim light of the Combat Information Center—illuminated at the moment only by a map display showing the entire continent of New Lanark—both men appeared drawn and haggard. The pale light made the circles under their eyes seem even deeper.

"It was bound to come to this eventually," Crow said. "The Senate and the Exarch knew it. Their only questions were who would attack and when—and whether Northwind could stand against the assault."

"They'll find out soon enough what the Highlanders are made of," Tara told him.

"Flesh and blood," Colonel Griffin said. He was pacing again, his hands clasped behind his back. "Entirely too much of which will have to be spilled, no matter what happens."

"Do we know yet if it's Radick who's brought the Wolves to this party?" Crow asked.

"They've been canny with their message traffic," Griffin said. "What little chatter we've managed to intercept doesn't refer to the Galaxy Commander by name, only by rank."

Tara shook her head. "That's not like Kal Radick. He likes his Bloodname too much to keep quiet about it."

"How sure are you of that?" Griffin asked.

"I'm not sure of anything," Tara admitted. "Except for this: The enemy is down on the surface of my world, they want it, and they can't have it."

Crow pointed to the map of New Lanark, where a mass of flashing red glyphs—the symbols for grounded DropShips, for known troop concentrations, and for observed 'Mech and vehicle types—clustered together on the salt flats west of the Bloodstone Range of the Rockspires.

"From where the Wolves are now," he said, "they can strike through the mountains here, at Red Ledge Pass, then take this city, and the rest of the world with it, in the space of a day. Our time to stop them may be measured in hours."

"Then we'll have to meet them here," Tara said. "Outside the city." She manipulated the screen to put a ring of blue light around the capital. "There's our line: just past weapons range from the built-up areas."

"It's going to take 'Mechs to stop them," Griffin said, still pacing. "And the Tyson and Varney rush retrofits only came out of the construction hangars the day before yesterday."

"How long will it take them to get from the factory to the battlefront?" Tara asked.

Griffin contemplated the map with the expression of a man doing sums in his head and not liking the answers. "Moving at full speed and abandoning any 'Mech that overheats and can't keep up the pace—a day and a half, minimum."

"We don't have a day and a half," Ezekiel Crow pointed out.

"We will," Tara said. "Colonel Griffin. Take whatever forces you need from the troops already on alert, and delay the Steel Wolves in Red Ledge Pass. Buy me thirty-six hours. That's all I ask."

Griffin halted in his restless pacing. "Thirty-six hours? You've got them." He saluted, turned, and strode from the Combat Information Center.

Crow turned to Tara. "You do know that you've probably just sent a man to his death," he said.

"More than one man," Tara replied. "But he'll do what he says. It's up to us to make sure that it won't all be for nothing."

PART FOUR

Northwind, Early Summer 3133
Forcing the Pass

26

Western slopes of the Bloodstone Range
Rockspire Mountains, Northwind
June, 3133; local summer

The sun had only been up for an hour, but already the salt flats were growing warm. The atmosphere on the flats was dry—bone-parchingly dry—and the wind that swept down off the distant mountains bore the smell of unfamiliar blossoms.

For Anastasia Kerensky, the arid, windswept landscape made a welcome change from the confined spaces of a DropShip, and long days spent breathing canned and stuffy shipboard air. Not everybody saw it that way—the specialists who worked the Steel Wolves' battlefield electronics were already grumbling about dust and corrosion—but Anastasia didn't care. She wouldn't be keeping her forces in a holding position on the salt flats long enough for it to matter.

For the moment, however, she had set up her command post in a large tent not far from the grounded DropShips. The tent was open on two sides, letting in the morning breeze while still providing shade. A portable map table was already up and running, its heavy power cords running from the tent to a humming generator nearby.

The grounded DropShips showed up on the map as dots of yellow, surrounded by clusters of other symbols, also in yellow, representing the various elements of the invasion force. This part of New Lanark had no cities or towns big enough to show up on the invasion map, but Anastasia knew that even in the howling wilderness there was always someone—a hermit trying his best to avoid civilization, or a naturalist looking for some new breed of bird or beast or insect, or just a pair of young lovers hoping to find a private place to pursue their further acquaintance.

One way or another, even if at a distance, the locals had to have seen the DropShips come down. Complete interdiction of ground-based communications was impossible. By now, the Prefect and her Northwind Highlanders would know where the Wolves had landed, and would be mustering troops to meet the threat.

The grumbling of engines ran underneath Anastasia's thoughts in a steady drone. She looked up for a moment and smiled at the sound: The tanks and artillery were disembarking now, growling out of the open maws of the DropShips and forming up into columns on the wide expanse of the salt flats.

She went back to looking over her maps. Inside another hour, at the most, the Steel Wolf BattleMechs would have left their berths aboard the DropShips and would be prepared for the march. The capital city of Tara lay a day away on the far side of the Rockspires. Her decision to avoid the main Tara DropPort had paid off so far, in that the Wolves hadn't taken any hits or losses to their DropShips on the way down.

The aerospace fighters she'd sent to keep the Highlanders too busy to take out the grounded DropShips weren't going to be so lucky. Some of them, perhaps most of them, would die. Still, they were doing a vital job, and they knew it; and for the survivors there would be honor, advancement, and an increased chance of having their personal genetic legacy carried forward through the Clan's breeding program.

Their morale, when they left for the attack, had been excellent. They would keep the Highlanders pinned down and distracted, spread out so loosely over the planet that the Prefect would never be able to gather them all in time.

Inside a day, Anastasia thought, she and her Wolves would be on the opposite side of the mountains, and within a half day more, the Fort at Tara would be hers.

The Highlanders would realize then that further resistence was futile. She could negotiate from a position of strength, or she could forgo negotiation entirely in favor of hunting the

Northwind armies down like rats, whichever she pleased.

While she was still thinking, she heard the sound of booted footsteps approaching, and looked up. It was Nicholas Darwin coming to join her, looking eager and alert. His uniform was clean and sharply pressed, the insignia of a Star Colonel fresh and gleaming, and he wore his cap tilted in the rakish tanker style. Anastasia paused a moment to regret that during the weeks on the DropShip she had not seized the chance to enjoy his company. Now that they were out in the field, her chances would be even fewer.

If Darwin shared Anastasia's regret for lost time he was not letting it show, anymore than she herself was. He paused the regulation two paces off, saluted, and said, "Galaxy Commander. The tanks and artillery are landed and ready. We await your orders."

"Excellent," said Anastasia.

She pointed to the display on the map table. A red line snaked through the mountains and out into the plains on the other side.

"Carve me a road," she said, "from here to Tara. The remaining infantry and the 'Mechs will follow as soon as they can—but you will have the responsibility of taking the lead. Go through the mountains and secure an assembly area for us on the plains north of Tara."

"Yes, Galaxy Commander," Darwin said. He saluted again and turned to go.

"Wait," Anastasia said. He halted, and she came around the table to stand next to him. Letting her accent slide downward into Tassa Kay's casual but friendly imprecision, she added, "Just one thing more."

Darwin turned back. "And that would be—"

"This," she said.

She took his face between her hands and kissed him deeply. Her left hand was still wrapped in a pressure bandage, a souvenir of her fight with Kal Radick, and her fingers felt stiff against the soft flesh of Darwin's cheek.

"When this campaign is over," she told him, "I am going to take over the Prefect's quarters—lock, stock, and pretty tartan sashes. And I am going to want somebody special to help me with staking my claim to the bed. So do not get killed if you can help it."

She released him then, and he stepped back.

"You certainly believe in incentives, Galaxy Commander," he said, and saluted once again before turning to leave the tent.

She watched, still smiling, as he strode over to the tank column assembly area and climbed to the top of his Condor tank.

"Warriors!" he called. His voice carried over the din of steel on steel and all the other sounds of DropShips unloading. "We have been given the honor of taking point on this operation. We drive east and south. Your orders are simple: find the Highlanders; engage them; destroy them. Speed is what Galaxy Commander Kerensky requires of us, and we will give it to her. Mount up. Follow me."

With that he dropped inside the turret of the tank. The mighty engines thundered to life, and the fifty-ton vehicle spun in place, its hoverjets working to point the tank's nose toward the jagged mountains looming gray blue on the horizon. From where she stood in the command tent, Anastasia could hear Darwin's voice coming over the tank's external speaker system: "On my command. Forward. Stand by. Execute."

At the command "execute," the hoverjets on the lead tank, and on the others drawn up behind it, impelled the vehicles into forward motion. The column of tanks and artillery headed eastward toward the distant mountains, quickly coming up to speed and eating up the ground at over sixty-five kilometers per hour—a spear, thought Anastasia Kerensky, cast to pierce the very heart of Northwind.

27

Eastern slopes of the Bloodstone Range
Rockspire Mountains, Northwind
June, 3133; local summer

The Northwind infantry was on the road again for the second time in as many weeks. The first time had proved to be a matter of "hurry up and wait." Will Elliot and his comrades had come tumbling out of their barracks in the predawn hours at their Sergeants' urgings, collected their weapons and equipment, and hastened onto transports—only to find themselves cooling their heels several hours later in holding camps that were, presumably, closer to where somebody in charge believed that the front lines might eventually be.

This time, Will thought, matters appeared more serious. Word had spread even before reveille that the Steel Wolves' DropShips had come down somewhere on the far side of the Rockspires, and nobody was foolish enough to think that the Wolves were going to stay where they'd landed. The encampment had boiled over into organized chaos at the news, and by breakfast time the mess tents were full of speculation. Will hadn't heard anything official yet, but it didn't take an old soldier to know that if the Wolves were down on Northwind then somebody would be going out to stop them.

He left the mess tent with his belly full of the comfort that came from hot tea and oatmeal porridge, and paused a moment to sniff the morning air. Here in the midst of the Highlanders' encampment in the Rockspire foothills, scents of fuel and torn earth predominated, but behind it all he could smell rain coming—not today, and probably not tomorrow, but before three days were out for sure. And if fighting in bad weather was anywhere near as bad as simply hiking and camping in it could sometimes be, then Highlanders and Wolves alike were in for an uncomfortable time.

An idea stirred into life at the back of his mind. It had something to do with how the instructors in boot camp had talked about showing initiative, but mostly it came from knowing that he'd driven every road and tramped along every trail in this part of the Rockspires, from the time he was old enough to be let out alone without a keeper.

He spotted his fellow scout/snipers Jock Gordon and Lexa McIntosh coming out of the mess tent and took it for a good omen.

"Hey," he said. "Jock, Lexa—come with me."

They joined him, Jock looking amiable and obliging as usual and Lexa—who was not as much of a trusting nature as her larger male companions—looking dubious.

"What's up?" she asked.

Will gestured toward the looming mountains, their lower slopes given a rosy tint by the early morning sun.

"Those hills are where I grew up," he said. "I used to earn my living at being somebody who knew his way around them. And now some Wolf Clan bastard thinks he's going to come through there and take over."

"I don't like it either," Lexa said. "But what's your point?"

"Point is, we're scouts. It says so right on our shoulder patches. Jock, do you think you could get us a vehicle—some kind of truck, or one of the Foxes if you can find one?"

"Without orders?" Jock asked dubiously. "Nobody's said we can—"

"Nobody so far has said that we can't, either," Will said. "As long as they don't, we're all right. I'm going to find the Sergeant, get the intel, then—"

The high-pitched warble of an announcement tone came over the air, followed by an amplified voice. "All troopers, form ranks, by unit. All troopers. . . ."

"Now's when they tell us what we can and can't do," said Lexa. She sounded disappointed.

"Damn," Will said. "Company quarters, then, and let's be sharp about it."

"Do you still want me to see about that truck?" Jock asked.

Will thought for a moment. "Go ahead. The two of you scrounge whatever you can and meet me at the assembly area. If they tell us we have to sit tight and do nothing, you can always take everything back and say that the Sergeant didn't want it after all."

"What Sergeant?"

"The one we're not asking permission from because he might say no if we did," Will said.

A sharp gust of wind blew up the loose dirt around him as he spoke. He tasted the earth, his native land. He didn't need a map of these mountains. If he could get out of camp, he could find the Steel Wolves no matter where they hid.

Feeling disgruntled, he made his way to the scout/sniper assembly area. Master Sergeant Murray was already there, watching the soldiers as they assembled.

"Private Elliot!" he said. "Good to see you. You're new, but all your instructors say that you're a promising lad."

"Yes, Sergeant," Will said. He kept his face blank, a useful skill in dealing with Sergeants, and one that he'd already possessed when he joined the infantry. Maintaining a straight face and keeping his private thoughts private in the company of wealthy, powerful, and frequently stupid wilderness tourists had been part of his job for years. "Thank you."

"Now here's the drill," Murray continued. "Find the Wolves. Engage, and report."

By now Will had been in the infantry long enough to understand that being thought promising by one's superiors was at best a mixed blessing—even, or perhaps especially, when their ideas coincided with one's own.

"That's it?" he asked.

"It'll have to be enough," Murray said. "We're understrength, and we're spread out all over New Lanark because we couldn't depend on the Wolves being polite and landing where we wanted them to. Now the first thing we need to know is what exactly we're up against. Who's out there, how many of them, where they are, where they're going. I know you paid attention in boot camp, so you know the drill."

Good thing the Sergeant doesn't know what I thought in boot camp, Will thought. Aloud, he said, "I have one of our lads I can send out looking for a vehicle. Is there any extra stuff that I can throw onto it?"

"We don't have much," Murray said. "Take what you need, but your main task involves rifles and radios."

"Got both of those."

A shout came from behind them, and the muted-windstorm sound of a hovercraft moving over loose dirt. Will turned and saw Jock Gordon pulling up with a Fox armored car. With its two front-mounted Voelkers 200 machine guns and its Diverse Optics Extended Range Medium Laser, the Fox was an excellent choice for a reconnaissance mission—far better than the toothless cargo truck Will had been expecting.

"I hope you signed a requisition to get that," Will said, mindful of the presence beside him of Master Sergeant Murray.

"I would have if anybody had been looking," Jock said.

"I'll mark it to you," Murray said. Will thought that the Master Sergeant looked amused. "Don't worry."

The Master Sergeant moved on. As soon as Murray was out of earshot, Lexa McIntosh emerged from around the corner of the nearest tent, carrying a heavy particle gun under one arm and dragging behind her a case of demolition charges that had to have weighed almost as much as she did.

"Got room in the Fox for this stuff?" she asked. "It's all I could find lying about loose."

"We'll make room," Will said. "We might find something that needs blowing up, and be glad that we brought it. Now we have to get going."

He swung himself onto the Fox's superstructure. "Mount up," he said. "Let's ride."

28

Red Ledge Pass
Bloodstone Range of the Rockspire Mountains
Northwind
June, 3133; local summer

By late afternoon, the Steel Wolves' tank column had penetrated the foothills of the Rockspires and had come to a temporary halt at the western end of Red Ledge Pass. So far the day had remained clear and warm, although the sky overhead was dotted with puffs and wisps of cloud in the "fish scales and mare's tails" pattern that hinted at a coming frontal passage.

In the old days of the HPG network—already taking on the flavor of a lost golden age, even in the minds of those who happily exploited the network's failure—a commander planning for an invasion could get up-to-date meteorological forecasts for battlefields light-years away from home. That luxury was gone now, possibly forever. Local weather knowledge had become once more the defender's advantage and the attacker's weakness.

The Steel Wolves' column had picked up a major multiple-lane highway running eastward from the salt flats, and had made good speed. Star Colonel Nicholas Darwin guessed that on a normal day, the road would be busy with both long-distance trucking and local traffic. More than once since this morning the column had passed rest stops and fueling stations, but the windows of all the buildings were dark, and the parking lots stood empty.

Clearly, word had spread across the plains even faster than the tank column could form up and deploy: *Lock your doors behind you and run—the Wolves are coming through!*

The same highway, if the road signs did not lie, continued on through the mountains, although the narrowness of the pass forced it to shrink from four lanes down to two. Darwin stood in the open turret of his Condor tank and looked from the signs to the map display generated by his handheld pad.

The display was based on imaging generated by the Wolves' own tracking and surveillance hardware during the DropShips' approach to Northwind, and was therefore reliable. On the other hand, the generated maps didn't come with route numbers and highway directions and conveniently labeled towns and villages, so there was always some difficulty matching up the terrain-as-marched-through with what the eyes-in-the-sky had reported.

If the locals were bright enough to change around the signposts before they ran away, as they sometimes were, the situation could get even more confusing. Fortunately for Darwin's tank column, the signpost at the mouth of the pass was a poor candidate for such an act of resistance. The information that this road was National Highway 66, and that it led—by way of the Bloodstone Range Protected Forest Area—to Liddisdale, Harlaugh, and Tara, was carved into the side of a massive red-rock boulder in capital letters twenty centimeters high.

No obliterating that one except with high explosives, Darwin thought in satisfaction. We are definitely on the right road. Now to make it all the way through. Because—he eyed the way in which the two-lane blacktop curved out of sight around a mountain shoulder not long after entering the narrow defile—if I were somebody trying to stop us, this is the sort of terrain I would pick to do it in.

He keyed on the mike for the tank column's command circuit. "Scouts and skirmishers out!" he ordered.

Up and down the column, armored troopers dismounted from the tracked or hover vehicles they'd been riding on. Having them proceed on foot would slow the column's pace considerably, but not nearly as much as it would be slowed if it got surprised by an enemy force and had no infantry out to meet the attack.

"We are going to have to keep up a smart pace if we're going to force the passage," the second in command of the column observed to

Darwin over the private circuit. Star Captain Greer had lost out to Darwin in the Trial of Position aboard *Lupus,* and had a tendency to be stiff about it from time to time. "Sir."

"I am aware of that," Darwin replied sharply. Greer could nourish his hurt feelings about having lost his Trial to a freeborn local half-breed on his own time. They were on Anastasia Kerensky's time now, and would not waste it. "But if it comes down to a choice between getting caught in the pass by nightfall and getting caught in the pass by the Highlanders—we will take our chances with the night, quaiff?"

"Aff," said Star Captain Greer. "Local sunset in two hours, sir."

"We will be running dark, with the sensors in high gain," Darwin said. "We have all done it a hundred times, and tonight is no different. Just like a drill, only with live fire."

"Sir." There was a brief pause; then Star Captain Greer spoke again over the command circuit. "All units report maps received and laid in, and the track set. On your command."

"Forward," Darwin said. "Pass to task group: 'Condition Red, weapons tight.' "

"Condition red, weapons tight, aye," Greer replied. "Moving out."

Engines roaring and rumbling back into life, the tank column growled forward into the mouth of the pass.

29

Western slopes of the Bloodstone Range
Rockspire Mountains, Northwind
June, 3133; local summer

In her command tent on the salt flats, Anastasia Kerensky gave the map table one last look. The yellow blips that represented Nicholas Darwin's armored column had moved some distance away from the symbols for the grounded ships. The hour was midafternoon, and the tank column was now at the pass.

It was time to set the main column into motion.

Anastasia left the map table to continue blinking and updating its display in solitude, and went out of the command tent. Her faithful *Ryoken II* 'Mech stood nearby, freshly repaired and repainted after the hard fighting on Achernar. She climbed the ladder up twelve meters to the *Ryoken*'s cockpit, entered and dogged the hatch behind her. With a well-practiced motion, she swung the activation bar down into a locked position and felt the fusion power plant rumble to life. Maneuvering herself in the small space, she settled into the 'Mech's command couch and strapped herself in. The controls that surrounded her were familiar extensions of her own body: footpedals for direction control and walking, throttle for speed, pressure-operated forearm joysticks for moving and twisting the torso, control for *Ryoken II*'s giant hands and for bringing her weapons to bear. Above all else was the neurohelmet that interfaced her brain and the 'Mech's gyroscope and musculature. Once she'd secured her helmet in place, she touched the control panel and recited her voice-identification code. The computer confirmed her identity and welcomed her home.

One quick glance confirmed weapons' status: all green. The customized short-range six packs on the *Ryoken*'s shoulders were Anastasia's preference over the standard LRM 15s. The 'Mech's torso bristled with medium lasers and, just below at the waist, PPCs, loaded and ready. The jump jets she'd added looked good as well. All was right; she expected no less.

She keyed on the speaker that would carry her voice to the various elements of her command.

"All units ready?"

"Ready, Galaxy Commander," came the reply over her helmet, from the most senior of the Star Colonels—Marks, it was, after the fiasco on Quentin had led to Ulan's disgrace. Like sound in a seashell, a rippling murmur of echoes ran around the circuit: *ready . . . ready . . . readyreadyready . . . ready.*

"I am leaving behind a strong defense with the DropShips," she said. "There is no shame in it; we will need the ships for Terra itself soon enough. Everyone else, follow me."

She wheeled her 'Mech around, pointing it toward the Rockspire Mountains and the pass through which Nicholas Darwin's troops should even now be heading. The *Ryoken* swung into motion easily, its great feet shifting, its armored hips twisting. She raised her hands as she sat in the cockpit, and the 'Mech's huge arms stretched skyward.

"The pace will be sustained," she said over the headset link. "Guide on me. I will keep it under redline, but only just under redline. Next stop, Tara."

And with luck, she thought, Tara will be in Tara. The coincidence of names made her snicker . . . Tara Tara Terra, she thought, take one and you have all three. I wonder what I should do with the Prefect when I catch her? Make her my bondswoman? Flog her and set her free? Execute her for failing to surrender in time? So many possibilities.

Anastasia's left hand throbbed beneath its bandages, a reminder of what she had done and endured before now to get this far. Power fantasies later, she decided. Action now.

She set the giant 'Mech to moving forward at a stroll, so that the inevitable heat buildup wouldn't overrun the cooling ability of the machine. The heavy and light tanks, spread out in a V-shape behind her, started moving forward at the same rate of speed. The diamond formation was good for fighting off air attacks—not that Northwind had much air capacity left after the Wolves' aerospace elements had finished savaging their atmospheric craft.

Nevertheless, it was always better to do the drill, so that if some other world should provide more resistance, the Steel Wolves would be ready for it.

30

Village of Liddisdale, Northwind
June, 3133; local summer

The afternoon was drawing on toward evening by the time Will Elliot and his two fellow scouts approached Red Ledge Pass along the main highway.

In the morning, and on through the early afternoon, they had passed a steady stream of vehicles and even foot traffic heading the other way. They had stopped one of the refugees—an elderly gentleman in an electric runabout, its backseat piled high with books, clothes, and a portable food cooler, its front passenger seat occupied by a parrot in a cage—to ask him if he had actually seen the Steel Wolf forces.

"Infantry—soldiers on foot, probably with Gauss rifles—or vehicles like this one, or tanks, or 'Mechs?" Will asked. "Anything like that?"

"I haven't seen anything," the old man said.

"There was a long-haul trucker screaming down Highway 66 at top speed just before dawn, telling everyone with a radio scanner that DropShips had landed on the salt flats. I think he'd seen them come down himself, and not just heard somebody else's message. Either way, I decided it was time to pack up the runabout and take Myrtle—" He nodded toward the caged parrot in the other seat. "—to some place where she'll be safe."

"Good idea," Will said. "Thanks."

The old man drove on toward Tara, and the three scouts continued westward into the foothills in the Fox armored car. By midafternoon the stream of refugees had diminished, and Will—who so far had found nothing else to occupy his mind—had begun to fret about his mother. She would have heard the same news as the old man with the parrot, but what would she do?

Mum wouldn't head for Tara, he didn't think. There was nobody there that she knew. And she wouldn't go to his sister across the mountains. That would mean heading straight into the Wolves' advance. Somewhere away from the main roads would be best, going back up into the mountains—Old Angus Macallan had a hunting cabin up on Razor Ridge, and would probably take her in if need be.

So would anybody else up there, if she wasn't too proud to ask, which she might be. He realized that he had no idea how his mother was likely to react in a crisis like this one. He wished he could make contact with her, make sure she had someplace to go, but he couldn't, not even on the public net. The Wolves might be listening—would surely be listening, if they were even half as clever as Will thought they were—and there was no way to guarantee that Mum wouldn't say something by accident that would reveal more than the enemy should know.

The scouts passed through Harlaugh in the late afternoon. The big lumber mill was silent and deserted, no plume of smoke rising from its tall smokestack. As they drove past, Will wondered briefly what his life would have been like if he'd taken a job there instead of talking with the recruiting sergeant. After a moment's consideration, he thought that he would probably have run off into the hills by now along with everybody else. He decided that he didn't like that idea; not running was better.

They reached Liddisdale at sunset. The fuel stop and the all-night pharmacy were both boarded shut—as if that would stop any determined soldiers on either side who wanted to get in—and nobody was in sight on the street or anywhere else. He thought he saw a curtain twitch in Bridie Casimir's house on the other side of the green, but he couldn't be sure. He hoped not; Bridie was a dreadful gossip, and had spanked him when he was six for digging up her garden in search of buried treasure—his sisters had sworn that she kept it hidden there, and he'd believed them—but she didn't deserve to get caught in the middle of an armored advance.

Jock Gordon broke the silence. "You're the

quiet one all of a sudden, Will. What's the story?"

"This is the town where I grew up," he said. He set the Fox armored car to hovering in place, and pointed at a big brick building, down the street two blocks off the central green. "See there? That's the secondary school. There's a chip in the stone steps out front where I set off a homemade incendiary device the night after graduation."

Lexa looked at him and shook her head. "And the judge called *me* a troublemaker."

"The difference is, I never got caught."

Jock nodded sagely. "Must be why the Sergeant put you in charge. For what we're doing, not getting caught at it is probably a good idea."

There was a moment of uncomfortable silence before Jock spoke again. "It's getting dark."

"You noticed," Lexa said. "And I hate to mention it, but the sensors on this bus have been intermittently fuzzing up ever since we passed that town back there with the big smokestack. I think maybe they're broken."

"They aren't broken," Will said. "The mountains in this district are full of magnetite and hematite. Iron ores."

Lexa slapped herself on the side of the head. "Bloodstone Range. Red Ledge Pass. Damn, I'm dumb—I should have guessed that magrez wasn't going to work well here."

"Cheer up," said Jock. "If you're dumb, the Wolves are probably even dumber."

Will nodded. "That's why sporting men in these mountains usually hire a professional guide. Not even a compass will help you out once the distortion gets really bad. And I don't think the Wolves have a guide along."

Lexa smiled evilly. "But we do."

"That's right," Will said. "And the first thing we're going to do now that we're here is get off the main road. The Wolves will be on it, I'm guessing—it'll be the one that's marked on the off-planet maps, and the one that'll show in any pictures they took from high up on their way in."

"What are you thinking we should use instead?" Jock asked.

"Unpaved logging roads," Will said. "Most of them won't appear on the satellite photos because they're hidden underneath the tree cover. People don't realize how thick the forest canopy around here really is. Every now and then somebody gets lost in these woods and nothing but a foot search stands a chance of finding them." He paused. "I found a guy once like that when I wasn't even looking for him. Of course, he'd been missing for two years by that point, so it didn't do him any good."

Lexa grimaced. "You're trying to cheer us up, aren't you?"

"Just letting you know what the Wolves are up against—and they don't even know it." He put the Fox back into forward motion. "Have your weapons charged and ready. If we don't know where the Wolves are yet—well, they could be anywhere."

31

Red Ledge Pass
Bloodstone Range of the Rockspire Mountains
Northwind
June, 3133; local summer

Star Colonel Nicholas Darwin stood in the open hatch of his Condor tank, scanning the winding road ahead. In actual combat, making a target of himself in such a manner would be dangerous, but the comparative safety of remaining buttoned up inside the vehicle was paid for with decreased visibility. The tanks had sophisticated on-board sensors and guidance displays, but the information they provided didn't satisfy him completely.

For this mission he wanted all the data that he could gather, and the feel for terrain that came from observations made using his own five senses. Small things—the shift of a breeze bearing a scent of oil or ozone, the disturbing flicker in his peripheral vision that meant something was moving and out of place, the taste of dust at the back of his throat—had given him warning before this, on other worlds. He wanted access to them now.

Behind him stretched out the long tail of vehicles and infantry that made up the advance column of the Steel Wolves. He wished that the column could move faster. Evening was drawing on, and the road already lay deep in purple shadow where the bulk of the surrounding mountains blocked out the sunlight. But however much he might wish it, he knew that faster progress was not possible. The column had to hold itself to the speed of its slowest members, or risk becoming scattered up and down the length of the narrow defile that was Red Ledge Pass.

Nicholas Darwin's command tank was at the head of the column. The only Steel Wolf units further along the road were the scouts—two- and three-person teams driving light, all-terrain Shandra Advanced Scout Vehicles and making frequent radio contact. He made a point of pulling the scouts back into the main group at regular intervals and sending out fresh teams to take their places.

Even among the Steel Wolves, people talked a lot of nonsense about scouts reporting contact with the enemy, but Nicholas Darwin knew as well as anyone else that such was not in fact the usual case. Most often, word of the enemy came when a scout failed to check in. He had done scout duty himself more than once before attaining his present rank. And he had even—more than once—found the enemy and lived to make his report, which had gained him a reputation early on for being both competent and lucky.

These days, however, he received reports, rather than making them. The Condor's radio crackled; he picked up the handset and keyed it on.

"Darwin here."

"Scout Team Alpha reporting, sir. Main road clear, next ten kilometers; no sign of the enemy."

Darwin checked the topographical map display on his handheld pad, and frowned. The main route—Highway 66, if the signs were to be believed—continued to follow the narrow defile through the pass. He did not like it. The column was strung out with no room to turn or maneuver, and the high mountains pressing in on either side of the road made him feel hemmed in and twitchy.

"What about off-road movement?" he inquired over the radio. "Can the column handle the rough terrain?"

"Negative, sir," said the distant, crackly voice. "The Shandras can handle it, and the 'Mechs could probably handle it, but nothing else. The grade is too steep."

"Very well," he said. "Continue checking out the terrain surrounding the road ahead. Pay particular attention to the high ground."

"Yes, sir."

"Anything further to report, Warrior?"

There was a pause. Darwin could imagine the distant infantryman frowning as he searched for the right words. "The sensor instrumentation on the Shandra, sir."

"What about the instrumentation?" Darwin experienced a sinking feeling. It was never good when previously reliable machinery started showing signs of unpredictable behavior. "What is it doing?"

"Bad readings, sir. Shifting, inconclusive, alerting when there is nothing to find."

"Any idea what might be going on?"

No pause this time. "Conjecture, sir. Signage earlier identified this part of the Rockspires as the Bloodstone Range, and I am seeing large outcroppings of hematite and magnetite ores. I believe these outcroppings to be interfering with the action of the sensors."

"Iron and lodestone," Darwin said thoughtfully. "Not surprising, Warrior. Place no trust in the sensors; rely on your own eyes and ears. Is that all?"

"Yes, sir."

"Good. Carry on. Let me know at once if you make contact with the enemy. Darwin out."

He closed the handheld and sealed it back into the cargo pocket of his fatigues. To the Condor's driver he said: "Move it on forward," then gave the hand signal for the rest of the column to follow.

Behind him, the long line of vehicles stirred into motion and rumbled onward into the gathering dusk.

32

Red Ledge Pass
Bloodstone Range of the Rockspire Mountains
Northwind
June, 3133; local summer

Will Elliot paused on the high ridge, just below the crest line. He took care to stand in the shelter of a large boulder so as not to show up against the darkening sky. Night was coming on, and the winding road below was already half in shadow.

The view was a familiar one. The last time he'd stood in this place, he'd just finished what turned out to be his last guiding job for Rockhawk Wilderness Tours. That day felt like a lifetime ago in some ways. The world around him had already been changing at that point, but he hadn't yet realized how fast those changes would come, or how many of them would be bad.

Here on the high ground the wind was keen,

cutting through his regimental jacket, making him wish that he had his old wilderness gear instead. Standard-issue summer uniforms did well enough for the warm weather in the low-lands, but hypothermia posed a danger all year round on the mountain slopes, and could kill an infantryman as dead as any Steel Wolf 'Mech. Jock and Lexa didn't understand the changeable mountain weather; he would have to keep an eye on both of them.

He scrambled back down the slope and into the shelter of the trees. The logging road wasn't far. It was a dirt track, not meant for the use of ForestryMechs. The 'Mechs were mostly good for clear-cutting, and for working the ordered rows of conifers and hardwoods on the big tree farms. Here in the protected forest area, any harvesting done would be selective and small-scale, the timber hand-cut with one- and two-person power saws and hauled out on skiploaders along narrow roads that left no visible scars on the mountainside.

The protected forests had survived largely because offworld tourists didn't like the big clear-cuts; and they didn't appreciate the presence of hulking ForestryMechs spoiling their pristine wilderness vistas. Will didn't know how much longer that concern for the mountains would endure, now that the offworld tourists were gone.

Except for the likes of the Steel Wolves, he reminded himself—and they aren't here to admire the scenery.

He was still in a somber mood when he joined Jock and Lexa by the Fox armored car.

"Bad news?" Lexa asked.

He shook his head. "No sight of the enemy yet."

"Maybe they're not coming," Jock said.

"They're coming," he said.

"There's a thousand miles around us in every direction," Jock said. "Why here?"

"Because Highway 66 is their best road through the mountains to Tara," Will said. "Further north there's Breakbone Pass, but that adds another two or three days to the trip even if the pass is clear—and I've known Breakbone to shut down for snow on the road as late as July or even August. Golden Gap to the south is a year-round road, but it's even farther out of their way than Breakbone. No, this is where they have to come through. Right here in Red Ledge Pass."

Unlike Jock, who was still looking dubious, Lexa appeared more eager than sensible. "Here? We fight them here?"

"No," Will said. "Here is where we leave the Fox. From this point on, we'll go on foot. A single man or woman is a lot harder to see in the woods than a machine."

Jock heaved his gear out of the back of the Fox. "And has a lot less chance of stopping a 'Mech."

Will shouldered his own pack and pulled his Gauss rifle out of the vehicle. "We don't have to stop 'Mechs. We spot 'Mechs, and we tell the people who *can* stop 'Mechs where to go find them. And we won't accomplish either one of those things by staying with the Fox."

"As long as we don't forget where we left it,"

Jock said. He was still rummaging through the supplies in the rear of the vehicles, including the box that Lexa had scrounged before they left camp. "Six blocks demo charge. Det cord. Gauss power packs and ammo. Right then." He put the items into his rucksack as he named them. "Where to now?"

"That way," Will said. He pointed back uphill to where red-tinged bareface, seeming to glow where it was touched by the setting sun, rose above the loose rocks and scrub conifers that covered the lower slopes. "Up in the saddle there, we can see down the pass in both directions. And that's the way the Wolves are going to approach, if they're being sensible."

"The Wolves?" Lexa asked. "If you ask me, the Wolves are crazy. If they were sensible, they wouldn't have bothered coming to Northwind in the first place."

"She has a point, Will," Jock said.

"Well, maybe they aren't sensible," Will conceded. "Just the same, if they're bringing vehicles through the mountains, they'll have to come along here. But us, we're walking. So we can go wherever we want."

"Then I want to go out for a drink," Lexa said.

"We'll have drinks together afterward," Will promised. "All three of us, and I'm buying the first round. But right now we have a job to do. The Wolves are going to have people ranging out ahead of their column and off the marked roads, doing the same kind of thing that we're doing. As soon as we run into one of those units, we'll know that the main body is coming up not far behind."

Jock said, "I hear that their infantry are some kind of specially bred supersoldier types."

"Elementals, they call them," said Will. "I saw a tri-vid special on them once."

"I wouldn't mind meeting one of them someday," Lexa said, in tones of lascivious curiosity. "On a purely social basis, that is."

"You'd like to meet *anybody* on a purely social basis," Jock said.

"I'll have you know I draw the line at pimps and lawyers . . . I wonder if the Wolves send those special-built guys out scouting, or do they save them for the big push?"

"It doesn't matter," said Will firmly. "We have one thing on our side that the Steel Wolves and their fancy custom-made supersoldiers don't."

"And that is?" asked Lexa.

"Local knowledge," Will said. "The Wolves are going to be navigating by offworld maps and scanned images taken from space. Their instruments aren't going to be much help to them once they get into the pass, and they don't have a trained wilderness guide along to show them the way and hold their hands during the frightening parts."

33

Red Ledge Pass
Bloodstone Range of the Rockspire Mountains
Northwind
June, 3133; local summer

The communications rig in Star Colonel Nicholas Darwin's Condor tank crackled into life. A moment longer, and Darwin heard the voice of the radar operator back at the DropShip landing zone on the salt flats.

"Negative sign of aircraft," the operator reported. "All quiet here at DropShip base."

Another voice came over the rig—Anastasia Kerensky, keeping a close eye on the armored column she had tasked with leading the way through the pass.

"Good," she said. "Keep it that way. These are your orders: If it flies, it dies."

Star Captain Greer spoke up over the column's private command circuit. "What are we expecting by way of resistance?"

"Not much," Darwin told his second in command. "Partisans at best. The available intelligence says that the Highlanders are unlikely to have any heavy 'Mechs—or 'Mechs of any kind—close enough to the pass to take up a blocking position."

"Are you certain of that intelligence?" Greer asked.

"Nothing is ever certain," Darwin said. "But I feel confident enough in it that I willingly cede to you the honor of going in first. Take point, full speed."

"Sir," Star Captain Greer replied, and his tank surged forward, passing Darwin's Condor—with some difficulty, since the road was narrow—to take up his new position at the head of the column.

"Trouble, Star Colonel," the sensor operator in Darwin's Condor said a few minutes later. "Our magnetic anomaly detectors are showing us nothing but garbage."

"The scouts predicted it," Darwin said. "All this red rock is magnetite and hematite ores, and they throw off the sensors. Run series checks and do your best to compensate."

"Yes, sir."

Darwin climbed back to the Condor's hatch and stepped so that his upper body protruded from the top of the vehicle. Risky, if a sniper was around, but with the sensors no longer functioning reliably, it was the only real way to see what was happening outside.

"Series checks show interference consistent with geologicals," the sensor operator said after a few minutes. "The receivers are acting correctly."

"Not a thing we can do about it, then," said Darwin.

"No, sir. But to the sensors, one heavy piece of metal is much like another. There is a chance that we could miss an enemy 'Mech in all this noise."

"If the enemy does have a 'Mech out there, it can only stay hidden so long as it does not fire its main weapons," Darwin said. "If the 'Mech fires anything, the signature will light up like sunrise on the infrared. Now pick up the pace. We have places still to go, and very little light."

"Will we be running at night, too, sir?"

"We will be, Warrior."

Nicholas Darwin surveyed the landscape around him. The sun had gone down behind the mountains already, and the evening was growing both dark and surprisingly chilly for the season. The wind that blew down from the mountaintops had passed over cold mountain streams, and over shaded snowbanks that might last all summer without melting. Those of his soldiers who had worn lightweight uniforms because of the heat on the salt flats would be shivering now. He hoped he didn't lose any of them to hypothermia and their own stupidity. The strike force could ill afford to take the loss.

"We will be," he said again. "We will run all day, all night, and all day again if we have to, until Northwind is ours."

34

Red Ledge Pass
Bloodstone Range of the Rockspire Mountains
Northwind
June, 3133; local summer

"Night's coming on," said Jock.

"So it is," Will said. He looked at the sky to the west, where blue was fast shading into indigo and the setting sun touched the clouds with crimson. "We'll have time enough to get up by Red Peaks before we have to show a light."

"I'm worried," Lexa said. "We haven't seen any fliers all day. None of theirs, none of ours."

"Could mean anything," Jock said. "Maybe they're mixing it up somewhere else."

"It could be that," Will said. "But if I had to guess a reason, I'd say that there was weather rolling in that the pilots don't want to fly through."

He gestured to the east, where thick clouds

darkened the sky almost to blackness. "See that?"

"I see it," Jock said. "But I'm a city lad myself. I couldn't say what it means."

"This time of year," Will said, "it means trouble. If I were still at my old job, right about now I'd be telling all the bold offworld hunters and fishermen to get ready to spend their weekend playing cards back at the lodge, because the best place to be in bad weather is snug under a roof."

"Too bad you can't tell that to the Wolves," said Lexa.

"Aye," said Will. "But if we meet any of them, I don't think we'll have the opportunity for talk. Not with words, at any rate. Maybe with rifles."

Lexa glanced at him curiously. "Have you ever shot anything? I mean, for real?"

"Just animals," Will said, at the same time as Jock said, "No."

"Me neither," Lexa said. She ran a hand over the stock of her laser rifle. "I know I'm good at the targets. But when it comes to the real thing . . . I don't know."

Will said, "When the time comes, we'll all do what we have to do. Remember, our primary orders are to make contact and report. Delaying the Steel Wolves comes extra."

"The three of us by ourselves aren't going to be able to delay anyone very much, anyway," Jock said.

"We'll do the best we can with what we've got," Will said. "Let's go."

They scrambled up the slope, with Will in the lead. The scrub conifers that grew at this altitude provided only scant cover, and the stones rolled under their feet, sometimes cascading downhill behind them.

"Don't skyline yourselves," Will reminded them as they approached the crest of the first slope.

"Don't worry," Lexa said. "We won't. Just because I like to shoot at targets doesn't mean I want to be one."

They paused just downhill from the crest line, and flopped belly-down on the dirt to crawl the last few yards. Will propped his binoculars in front of his eyes.

"See anything?" Jock asked.

"Nothing moving."

For a while they watched the road below in silence. Then Lexa said, "All this waiting and watching is just grand, but you'd think that there'd be something else we could do."

"I know what you mean," Will said. "But first let's get a little farther east."

They crawled backward down from the skyline. Then they walked along the ridge, ten yards below the crest, for close to three kilometers, until Will said, "Here. This is the best place to watch the road."

"I can't see anything from here," Lexa complained. "It's getting too dark."

"Listen for the noise of birds being disturbed. They'll fly up from the woods. Look for smoke or dust."

"And look for gunfire," Jock added. "The

Wolves are going to be out there looking for us at the same time as we're looking for them. They don't have a trusty native guide, either, so they're going to believe that anything that so much as rustles in the underbrush is a Highlander scout patrol."

"That's exactly what I've been thinking," Will said. "Which gives me an idea about what we can do with all that explosive firepower you've been hauling around in your backpack."

"And what's that?"

"How big is the biggest 'Mech you know?"

"I've heard that the *Jupiter* 'Mechs are twelve meters tall," Jock said. "I've never seen one of 'em, though."

"Doesn't matter. Twelve meters tall would give it a stride of about five meters." Will paced out the dimensions of a single giant step. "Give me a piece of rope. Great. Those demolition blocks you've got with you—measure out the footprints of a *Jupiter*. Lexa, use your laser rifle to drill holes down to rock so Jock can put in the charges. Separate detonators for each charge."

"I believe I know what you're planning," Lexa said. She unlimbered her laser rifle and aimed it down at the rock. "And you're a mean, mean man. I like the way you think."

35

Red Ledge Pass
Bloodstone Range of the Rockspire Mountains
Northwind
June, 3133; local summer

"Star Colonel."

Nicholas Darwin looked down at the sensor operator from his position in the open hatch of the Condor tank.

"What is it, Warrior?"

The sensor operator wore a set of heavy earphones. At the moment he was holding one of the padded earcups away from his head so that he could hear his commanding officer's reply. "We have picked up something of interest on seismic, sir."

"What kind of interest?"

"We are no longer getting useful data on electromagnetic out here—there is too much iron in these hills. But, sir, listen to this."

He pulled off the headset and handed it up to Darwin, stretching out the connecting cable so that his commanding officer could put on the headphones and listen without having to climb back down into the belly of the tank. Darwin settled the headset onto his own head, and adjusted the cups over his ears.

The sensor operator hit the replay button on his console, and Darwin could hear it—the sound that ruled the battlefield. Footsteps. Big footsteps. The footsteps of something heavy enough to shake the very ground when it walked.

A BattleMech.

"Did any of the other sensor units pick this up?" Darwin asked as soon as the replay was done.

"Aff, sir. Scout Team Beta, with the Shandra scout vehicle four kilometers to the north. We are comparing signals now, sir, and—"

The sensor operator paused and touched the display screen.

"There it is, sir. Range twenty, due west of our position, moving from south to north at forty-five kilometers per hour. We are getting separation, and a good triangulation."

"Very well," Darwin said. "Do you know where it stopped?"

"Aff, sir."

"Chart it and transmit that location to all units. With that size and speed, it could be an *Atlas* or even a *Jupiter*. If it starts moving again, let me know."

"Sir."

Darwin turned back to his tactical comms. "All units, enemy 'Mech located. We are going to take this one. Arm with long-range armor-piercing."

The other commanders acknowledged.

Darwin smiled. Now that he had the Highlanders' 'Mech located, he would be able to take it out with a sudden, overwhelming blow.

"Forward," he said. "We will salvo on target when in range."

Anastasia Kerensky would be pleased.

On the cliff top by the saddle between the mountains, time passed slowly. Will, Lexa, and Jock took turns watching the road to the west through infrared binoculars. The night air grew cooler around them as they waited, and the wind made sighing noises in the conifers on the slope below.

"What happens if you guessed wrong?" Lexa asked, after nothing had happened for some time.

"Then some other scout team will get the glory," Will said. "But I don't think—"

"I see something," Jock called down from his position lying belly-down on the ridge, the binoculars to his eyes.

"What?"

"Heat shimmer. Bearing zero-seven-five true."

Will and Lexa crawled up onto the ridge to lie beside Jock and look out through their own binoculars at the road below.

"I see it, too," Lexa said. "But something—

tell me. Do you think they heard our little sound show?"

"I certainly hope so," Will said.

"And if they heard it," she persisted, "then they know where that supposed 'Mech of ours is?"

"Can't bet that they don't," Jock agreed.

"Then about thirty seconds after they get in range, we're going to get hit hard."

Will thought a moment. "You're probably right. Do either of you know the max range of the Steel Wolves' biggest?"

"Their best bet for capturing a 'Mech would be infantry," said Lexa. "And that means a range of—ah, damn, I knew I should have stayed awake more during basic training—no more than a hundred meters."

"That's no good," Jock said. "They can't afford the time to send up the gorillas. It'll be rockets."

36

Red Ledge Pass
Bloodstone Range of the Rockspire Mountains
Northwind
June, 3133; local summer

The report came back to Nicholas Darwin from the sensor operator in his Condor tank: "Target in range."

"Very well," Darwin said. "On my command . . . stand by . . . fire."

Columns of smoke and fire lit up the night sky to the right and to the left of Darwin's tank and arced away to the east, as the Valiant Arbalest long-range missiles of all the Steel Wolves' Condor tanks spoke as one. The multiple separate columns first converged in the darkness of midheaven, then slowly descended to a point. That point suddenly grew brighter, like an expanding ball of incandescent gas.

Nearly a minute later the sound of rolling thunder came echoing from the distant hills.

"Well," said Star Captain Greer over the private command circuit, "if the Highlanders somehow failed before to notice that we were coming, they certainly know it now."

"They were bound to find out," Nicholas said. "And they have found out in the worst way—by losing a 'Mech. Move out now. Resume tactical column."

The order echoed through the links.

"Losing signal," the communications operator said. "Sir, the radio propagation is terrible through here."

"It will only get worse," Nicholas said. "Pass to all units: Continue west, do not allow the Highlanders to slow you down. Maintain visual contact with the friendly beside you."

We have an appointment to keep on the far side of the mountains, he added to himself. He would not let Anastasia Kerensky down.

"Forward, Wolves!"

The road to Tara lay through the black shadows in the valleys of Red Ledge Pass. Ahead, smoke rose from just below the crest of a ridge.

"Our orders were to locate the enemy and report," Jock said.

"We've done that," Lexa said. She was sitting on the hood of their vehicle, some three kilometers back from where an empty bit of ridge line had recently become smoking vapor. "I thought that sound was going to blow out my eardrums."

"Just be glad that their aim was good," Will said. "A miss could have nailed us all the way over here."

"And I suppose you thought about all that in advance," she said.

"No, not really," Will admitted. "I didn't think of it until after we popped those fake footsteps."

Jock nodded soberly. "So do you know which way they'll be coming?"

"Yes . . . well, no. Not exactly. I have a best guess, though."

"Why not radio it in?" Lexa asked.

"Because for one thing, radio reception is no good through here," Will said. "And for another thing, we don't want the Steel Wolves listening in when we make our report."

"Then we'd better hope that someone with landline communications saw the explosion and called it in," Jock said.

Lexa glanced upward at the night sky as Jock spoke. "They may have done better than that," she said.

There was a whistling sound, and a momentary darker shadow passed across the night. A second later, a man in powered jump armor marked with the insignia of the Northwind Highlanders scooted out of the sky.

"What was that flash and bang?" he demanded as soon as the dust of his landing had cleared. "I've been assigned by Colonel Griffin to scout forward and find out what the hell."

"Well, you can take this back with you to the Colonel," Lexa said. "We have the Wolves located. They're out to the west of this spot, somewhere in missile range, and they're down one rack of ammo per long-range shooter."

"Anything else?"

"Yes," Will said. "They're coming through the mountains on Highway 66."

"Great," said the man in jump armor. "I'll take that word back to the Colonel. Oh, one more thing. Better be careful. I was told they've got a hell of a big 'Mech, and it's not too far from here. Have you seen it?"

"Seen it?" Lexa asked. She laughed. "We *are* it."

37

Red Ledge Pass
Bloodstone Range of the Rockspire Mountains
Northwind
June, 3133; local summer

"Better you than me," said the infantryman in jump armor. "I'll take your message back to the Colonel."

"Thanks," said Will.

"And if I were you I'd be moving out of here soon. There's probably going to be hell's own horde of Wolves coming through here before very long."

Will nodded. "Sure."

The infantryman in jump armor took off, rising from the ground in a long flat arc. The jets of his suit made a fast-fading blaze of light against the night sky. A distant observer, knowing no better, might have taken it for the path of a meteor.

Will and his two companions watched his departure in silence. Lexa was the first to speak.

"He's right. We should go. But—"

"Aye," said Jock.

Another drawn out silence followed. Finally Will said, "I think we ought to get at least a look at the Wolves before we run."

"Yeah," said Lexa. "I think we should."

"Aye," said Jock again. "But how are we going to do it?"

"Same as before," Will said. "We take the Fox as close as we can without getting burned; then we get out and walk." He thought further, and added, "One of us'll have to wait on the road with the Fox's hover jets running. We might need to get out in a hurry."

Lexa and Jock nodded agreement to the plan, such as it was, and they soon had the Fox armored car back on the road. With Jock at the wheel, they drove to within a few hundred meters of the timberline. At that point the road ended except for a footpath—not much more than a blazed trail, and one that would have been useless in the dark if Will hadn't known the way.

Will took his Gauss rifle from the Fox. Lexa hesitated briefly, then set aside her laser rifle in favor of the heavy particle gun she'd brought with her that morning.

"More firepower," she explained.

"Can't hurt," Will agreed. "Jock, you get the armored car pointed back down the way we came, and keep it warmed up and ready to go."

Lexa and Will took the footpath up to the timberline and across the bareface, then belly-crawled the last few meters. Will said, "This is as far as we ought to go. Any nearer the road and we'll be out of cover. We're looking at a blind turn down there as it is—anyone coming through won't actually be within range until we're almost on top of them."

"Maybe you're looking at a blind curve," said Lexa. "For all that I can see, this entire mountain is as dark as the inside of a goat."

"I've been here before. That's the secret. I used to take parties of rock climbers through Red Ledge in the summertime, back before the HPG net went down and the offworld tourists stopped coming."

"You're kidding. Rock climbers?"

"God's honest truth," said Will. "The road's about fifty meters ahead of us and fifty meters down, and the walls of the pass at that point are bare rock and go straight up. The rock climbers liked the challenge. They'd spend all day pulling themselves up the cliff face by their fingernails, and I'd go around by the trail and meet them at the top with a nice hot dinner."

"I wish someone would meet us with a nice hot dinner," said Lexa. "Are you sure we don't want to get a bit closer? We aren't going to get a real good look from here."

"This is close enough. We'll hear the Wolves a long time before we ever get a chance to see them."

Time passed. With the sky covered in clouds, Will found it hard to estimate hours and minutes. He considered illuminating the face of his watch long enough to check, but reminded himself that an enemy sniper would only need one flash of light in the dark to pinpoint his location. After a while, he became aware of a low, almost subliminal rumbling—a distant noise that was almost more a shuddering in the ground and a tremor in the air than anything actually heard.

"Here they come," he said. "Sounds like they're pushing it."

"Top speed, in the dark? Somebody sure has guts."

"Nobody ever said the Wolves were cowards," Will said.

"Not more than once, anyway," Lexa agreed. "This bunch—how many of them are there, do you think?"

He shrugged, though he knew she couldn't see the movement in the dark. "Can't tell. Some kind of advance guard, probably—a noise like that isn't just a couple of scouts." A moment later he continued, moved by the same impulse that earlier had rendered him unwilling to turn tail without actually making visual contact with the advancing Wolves. "I think we can throw a scare into them, though—maybe get them to slow down a little."

"How?"

"Let them come closer. Get the particle gun ready, and when I give the word, blast away with it against that cliff face I was talking about earlier. Try to hit it about twelve meters off the ground. Can you do that in the dark?"

Lexa chuckled. "I can do a lot of things in the dark, soldier. Hitting a rock wall isn't even going to be one of the tough ones."

They fell silent again. Will heard Lexa unlimbering the particle gun and settling down into a prone firing position. He had his own Gauss rifle close to hand. The rumbling of the Wolves' advance grew closer, growing from a faint and steady noise to an enormous and overwhelming one.

Closer, Will exhorted the Wolves privately, as the air filled with the noise of engines and tank treads. Come just a little closer. Just a little more. . . .

"Now."

He fired his Gauss rifle at random into the dark. Beside him, at the same time, Lexa let fly with the particle gun.

The weapon roared. Its blast hit the red stone of the cliff with a noise of splitting rock, and illuminated the sheer bareface for an instant with a yellow light brighter than the day. Rock shards flew about in all directions like broken glass.

"Time to go now, I think," Will said as the echoes died. "Leave the Wolves to stew."

38

Red Ledge Pass
Bloodstone Range of the Rockspire Mountains
Northwind
June, 3133; local summer

Nicholas Darwin's Condor tank lurched and grumbled along the highway—the narrow two-lane road, to give it a more accurate description—leading along the bottom of Red Ledge Pass. The tank's hatch was closed, since in the dark night there was no advantage to leaving an observer exposed to possible enemy fire.

The Condor's interior dimensions left little room for movement; tankers couldn't afford to be claustrophobes. Darwin watched the display screens from a position bare inches away from the sensor operator's shoulders.

Garbage and more garbage, he thought in frustration. His own eyes were blinded by the night and the clouded sky, and the sensors that should have augmented or replaced them gave back nothing but bad data—all of it rendered contradictory, fragmentary, or garbled by the high concentration of iron ores in the mountains that hemmed them in on all sides.

At least the road leading through Red Ledge Pass was open and clearly marked. All that the tank column had to do was stay on it, and overwhelm all opposition along it, and in time they would reach the far side of the mountains. And after the mountains, the capital.

The tank's communications rig broke the silence with its wheebling signal. The comms operator listened over the headset, then turned to Darwin.

"It is a general communication, sir."

"Put it on."

The operator toggled the switch. A voice crackled. Bad interference, thought Darwin, those damned rocks again.

"Command," said the crackling voice, "this is Scout Team Delta."

"Go ahead, Delta."

"I wish to report that we have made contact with the enemy."

"Excellent," Darwin said. "What is their position?"

"Transmitting encoded grid coordinates now, Star Colonel." There was a pause, filled with a burst of crackles and high-pitched whistling. "There is one unanticipated problem, sir."

"What is it, Delta?"

"That *Jupiter* 'Mech we thought we had finished off, sir? It appears to still be functional.

The Highlanders have it holding the pass with infantry support just ahead of us."

Damn, thought Darwin. Our long-range missiles failed to take it out . . . which means that it waits for us in an entrenched position.

He was careful not to let his expression reflect his chagrin. "You are sure of this?"

"Aff, sir. It discharged its main weapon once while Delta was scouting within several meters of its position. I saw the flash myself."

"You are coolheaded, Warrior. You did well."

"Thank you, sir. What do we do now?"

"Hold your position. Do not attack unless ordered. Darwin out."

He frowned, still thinking. Damn. He most emphatically did not want to take on an entrenched *Jupiter* BattleMech and its infantry support, not in a narrow pass in the dark. Not when all the advantage lay with the defenders.

To the communications officer, he said, "Pass the word to the entire column: Stand down. We will tackle the enemy 'Mech at first light." He waited while the signal went out, then said, "Open a channel to Galaxy Commander Kerensky."

Once again the communications rig crackled and wheebled, and he heard the familiar clear ringing tones, only slightly distorted by the transmission. "Galaxy Commander Anastasia Kerensky here."

"Star Colonel Nicholas Darwin here. We have a report from the advance scouts. The enemy are holding the narrowest part of the pass with a *Jupiter* BattleMech, and—unless otherwise directed—I do not intend to squander personnel and equipment trying to take it out in the dark. If we had moonlight, it might be possible. But we have clouds tonight, and no moon."

This time there was a long pause. Darwin could imagine Anastasia Kerensky's frustrated expression, her restless pacing, while she swallowed the bad news. If she asked him to press the attack, he would do so—she was the Galaxy Commander, and a Kerensky, and what she ordered, the Wolves would do.

Finally, once again, he heard Anastasia's voice. "Understood, Star Colonel. Stand down for the night."

39

The Fort
City of Tara, Northwind
June, 3133; local summer

The Highlanders' Combat Information Center lay deep within the hardened bombproof recesses of the Fort. Ordinary residents of Northwind's capital city might be frightened out of their sleep by the intermittent flashes and rumblings that came from the direction of the DropPort, where local aerospace defense fighters contended with the Steel Wolves for control of the skies. Down in CIC, however, neither light nor sound could penetrate. Only the flicker of display monitors and the hiss and slide of message printouts falling into receiving trays gave any hint that somewhere outside a battle was raging.

Tara Campbell had been in CIC since before the Steel Wolf DropShips had landed, living on stale sandwiches and mugs of strong sweet tea and listening to the battle reports as they came in. She knew that the figures and the dry summaries didn't tell it all. Men and women were dying, burning like meteors across the sky above the DropPort; and miles away in Red Ledge Pass, Steel Wolves and Highlanders confronted each other in the dark.

She wished for a moment that she was out there with the troops holding the pass, and that Colonel Griffin had been the one left behind in bombproof safety. She knew from experience that it was much easier to be a junior officer, or even a Colonel, out in the field. Your only worry then was the enemy directly in front of you. A Prefect, on the other hand, had to worry about everything: the Wolves in the pass, the retrofitted 'Mechs still in the factories, the reserve air cover that had yet to be scraped together from God-knew-where.

The door to the Combat Information Center sighed open, breaking into her exhausted thoughts and admitting Ezekiel Crow. The Paladin was clean-uniformed and freshly shaven. If Tara hadn't known for a fact that he'd been awake almost as long she had, those minor changes would have done a surprisingly good job of convincing her that he'd shown up alert and well-rested after a full night's sleep.

Paladins, too, had to worry about everything.

"Countess," he said, by way of greeting.

Her answering nod was formal and correct, a triumph of training over exhaustion. "Paladin."

"What's the status?"

"The Wolves aren't packing up and going home. But we knew that already." She mustered enough energy for a smile—the troops, after all, were watching. "The good news is, they seem to have halted for the night."

Crow came over to join her at the map of Red Ledge Pass displayed on the planning table. The red lights that marked known and conjectured enemy units hadn't moved in over an hour; she couldn't remember whether they'd advanced at all while the Paladin had been away from CIC.

Now he studied the map gravely and said, "Rather than trying to force a narrow road in the dark? I'm not sure that I blame them. What they lose in time, they'll make up for in daylight by being well-rested."

"You really know how to cheer a woman up, my lord."

He shook his head regretfully. "Heartening lies aren't what's called for at the moment, I'm afraid."

"Damn. Because I've run out of good ones to tell myself." She gestured at one of the workstations, currently attended by a young woman in regimental fatigues—Corporal Baker, according to her name tag. "Meteorology is starting to make unhappy noises about weather patterns to the southeast of here. We could end up fighting in the rain, or worse."

Crow considered the meteorology screen and the map table, and nodded gravely. "True enough. On the other hand, all that low cloud cover seems likely to discourage attack from the air."

"Good." The Clan Wolf aerospace fighters had been yet another factor delaying the combat readiness of the converted Construction- and MiningMechs. Moving the new battle machines out of the factory and into the streets of the city would make them into easy and convenient targets if the Wolves' air wing wasn't neutralized first. "Once the skies are safe—"

She fell silent, twisting a strand of her hair around her forefinger as she tried to estimate the point when local air support would have inflicted enough damage on the Wolves that the converted 'Mechs could roll out without taking too many losses. The answer eluded her—the part of her brain that normally handled such calculations with ease was fogged by lack of sleep.

She felt the light touch of a hand on her forearm, and suppressed a start.

Turning her head, she saw that the hand belonged to Ezekiel Crow. The Paladin looked concerned, causing Tara to wonder exactly how much exhaustion she herself betrayed to an outside observer, if the visible signs of it could worry him.

"Prefect," he said. "A word with you in private?"

Translation, she thought, let's not disturb the rank and file with this discussion. She nodded and followed Crow out into the empty, dimly lit corridor.

As soon as the door closed behind them, he turned to face her, stopping just inside casual speaking distance—not close enough that a chance passerby might notice and remark on it, but still a change from his usual punctilious formality. This close, she could see the lines of fatigue marking his face, and not even the natural tan of his complexion could hide the dark circles under his eyes.

When he spoke, his voice was blunt but kind. "Countess, you will be of no use to Northwind tomorrow if you don't get some sleep tonight."

"I shouldn't leave CIC—"

"Let me take over that duty." He gave her a wry smile. "A Paladin will function as well as a Prefect for reassurance and inspirational purposes, at least for an hour or so."

The thought of getting some rest was tempting, but she felt obliged to give resistance one more feeble try. "You need sleep as much as I do."

"I caught a quick nap in my office earlier—not much, but sufficient. You need to go do the same."

She was still reluctant, but when she found herself struggling to smother a yawn even as she stood there, she gave in. "All right. But only for a couple of hours. And call me at once if anything changes."

"Of course," he said, and stepped back inside CIC.

She didn't bother going to her quarters in the New Barracks. They were too far away. If she was going to take an hour or so off for sleep, she didn't want to waste any of it.

Her office—the small temporary office down

here in the depths, rather than the personal office in her quarters or the large formal office several levels above her head in the Fort proper—contained a couch, an elderly specimen that might have been intended for the comfort of visitors, but more than likely was meant to be used as she was planning to use it now. She half dropped, half fell onto the cracked green leather cushions, not bothering to loosen her clothing or take off her shoes, and was asleep within seconds.

40

Eastern slopes of the Bloodstone Range
Rockspire Mountains, Northwind
June, 3133; local summer

The first light of the rising sun touched the eastern foothills of the Bloodstones with a wash of pink. Colonel Michael Griffin awakened at the change in the light; he'd finally caught an hour or so of sleep along toward dawn, wrapped in a sleeping bag on a cot set up by the foot of his *Koshi*. If the Steel Wolves' attack came under cover of night, he didn't intend to waste his time running for the 'Mech in the dark. He hadn't really expected to be awakened instead by the sky above him paling toward daylight, and the sound of reveille playing over the encampment's speakers.

"Tea, sir?"

His aide-de-camp, Lieutenant Owain Jones, approached the cot with a steaming mug in either hand. Griffin sat up, accepted one of the mugs, and drank gratefully of the strong, heavily sweetened contents.

"Thank you, Lieutenant."

"You're welcome, Colonel." The early summer mornings at this elevation were chillier than those back at base. Jones—another warm-climate native, like Griffin himself—had his hands wrapped around the mug for warmth as he drank. "So the Wolves didn't come in the night, after all."

"Don't worry, Lieutenant. Now that it's daylight, they'll be on the move for sure."

"For what we are about to receive," said Jones, "may the Lord make us truly thankful. How do you rate our chances of stopping them?"

"We don't have to stop them. Just hold them."

"For how long?"

"Until I tell you it's been long enough," Griffin said, and handed back the empty mug.

Lieutenant Jones faded away toward the mess tent, leaving Griffin thoughtful. He had time, he estimated, for catching a quick breakfast and tending to those early-morning personal chores that couldn't be handled gracefully in the cockpit of a 'Mech. Then he would have to make an address to the troops. He couldn't say much more to them than he had to Lieutenant Jones, but everyone would expect him to say something, even if they mocked his words later in private. Morale would suffer if he didn't behave as expected.

After that, there would be nothing to do but climb into the *Koshi* and wait.

Two hours later, he was still waiting. The 'Mech, with its height of eye, gave him a good view of the plain and of the disposition of his forces, a view augmented by the symbolic map display projected in the *Koshi*'s cockpit.

Nothing showed up yet on actual visual, but the map display was already providing useful information. The scouts' reports on the Wolf armor put their last confirmed location far back down the main road leading through the pass: On the display, the armored column showed up as a series of solid red lines. Their assumed position—dotted red lines showing where the column might currently be, given the known top speed of the reported units—was considerably closer.

Nearer still on the projected maps were the blue lines of Griffin's own units, a few of them actually visible from the cockpit of his 'Mech. The bulk of them showed up only on the map, either because they occupied positions outside his line of sight or because they were concealed or under cover.

He could have wished for a better mix of units; what he had, while the best that the Countess and the Paladin could spare from organizing the main defenses, was far too light for his taste—mostly infantry, trained but unseasoned in combat. For support, he had self-propelled artillery in the center, missile-launchers on the flanks, and himself, in the *Koshi*.

The range of their weapons was marked out in pale blue on the map display, and their maximum sensor range in blue of an even paler shade. At some point the advancing pale pink of the assumed Steel Wolf formation—a formidable force, even if the scouts' reports had been exaggerated by a factor of ten—would intersect with the pale blue. The resulting purple areas would show the locations of possible attack.

Then the sensors would make contact. . . .

"Sir," Lieutenant Jones's voice came over the *Koshi*'s communications system. "Reply to your message to headquarters. The Prefect says, 'Buy me time.' "

"There's only one place today that's selling it," Griffin said. He looked again at the map, keying up the names of the units forming the heavy blue line that blocked egress from the mountains into the open plains that lay to the north of the capital city. "And I know what coin we have to use."

"Nobody's ever said that Highlanders don't know the value of money," Jones said. "If we have to pay, we'll drive a hard bargain first."

"Rest assured, Lieutenant, I'll pinch every penny. But for now, it's a waiting game."

He ran down the weapons systems in his *Koshi*. Short-range missiles in the right arm, systems green. Check. Ammo full. Short-range missiles, left arm, systems green. Check. Ammo full. Active probe and target acquisition. Check, and check. Jump jets, ready, on line. Cooling max.

Reactor in hot standby. Confirmed—everything was good to go.

With that taken care of, he began pacing along the defensive line that he had drawn up earlier, checking the lines of sight. With nothing but short-range missiles on board, he didn't dare use the *Koshi* to take on the tank killers that the Wolves had in the lead. The 'Mech's armor was good, but a lucky shot could still take it out . . . a lucky shot that would be more likely if the enemy could shoot at will without fearing countering fire.

He paced back to where a rocky outcropping shielded him from the front, and where his line of sight into the valley put everything within view in his range.

"Pass to all units," he said on the command circuit. "We're going dark. No active sensors. No electromagnetic communications from here out. Passive means only. Make the bastards guess where we are."

"Why? What are you planning?" Jones asked.

"They'll get here and we'll fight them, whether they come early or late," Griffin explained. "But why advertise where we are exactly? They can detect our sensors twice as far as our sensors will show us where they are. If they don't know where we are, they'll have to advance more slowly because we could be anywhere."

"Right," Jones said. "Well, I'll stick close by you when the action turns hot."

"You do that," Griffin told him.

Lieutenant Jones was in a BE701 Joust tank, the better to keep enemy infantry off of Griffin's 'Mech. A single trooper couldn't do much against one of the big fighting machines—but infantry never came singly, that was the problem. They came in squads and platoons and companies, and enough of them in one place could swarm over even the biggest 'Mech like a cloud of maddened insects.

"Stay close," Griffin said, "but stay behind me. Lots of stuff is going to be flying out the front, and I don't want you to get in the way."

"No worries there," Jones said.

The light blue area on the display map faded back as the Highlanders' active sensors switched off, leaving Griffin with still more unknown ground to fret about. The pale pink of the projected Wolf advance inched forward.

Time crawled by.

Griffin checked the chronometer in the 'Mech's cockpit repeatedly, when he wasn't scanning the land and the sky. The sun was well up by now, although clouds still lowered above the mountain peaks. More clouds gathered on the horizon behind him to the south and east—the bad weather that Meteorology had been predicting for some days now, though it wasn't likely to arrive in time to interfere with his plans for the day.

On the map display, the pink mist of the Wolves' possible position by now had met the blue mist of the Highlanders' passive sensor range, and in some places had even met the darker blue of weapons range. Still, there were no contact reports.

No firing.

Nothing.

Michael Griffin waited.

41

Red Ledge Pass and the eastern Bloodstone foothills
Rockspire Mountains, Northwind
June, 3133; local summer

The morning sun burned through the clouds hanging over the narrow road through Red Ledge Pass. During the hours of darkness Nicholas Darwin had rested as best he could in the narrow confines of his Condor tank. Now he stood once again in the Condor's turret, with the Steel Wolves' armored column waiting for orders behind him like a hunting beast on a tight chain.

The feel of the air had changed in the night; even a city-bred offworlder like himself could sense the difference. The storm from the southeast that the meteorologists had fretted about was definitely coming, and he had to force the pass and take out the Highlanders' resistance on the other side while the current weather held. The last thing Anastasia Kerensky needed was for her main tank column to get caught in a canyon during a flash flood.

The overnight delay had been bad enough. He should have taken Northwind's capital city by now, or at least have been closing in on it. Instead, he was still looking at peaks on either side and narrow passes ahead of him—and to his frustration, the 'Mech that had stopped the column for the night had pulled out sometime in the hours before sunrise, denying him and his troops the satisfaction of taking it down.

Now, damn it, that same 'Mech probably waited for them somewhere on the road ahead, ready to do its damage in daylight this time. Well, let it wait. Darwin was ready for it.

Anastasia Kerensky would reward success. He had no doubt but that she would reward failure, too—and he did not need that kind of reward.

"Forward," he ordered. "Do not stop for anything."

"What do we do if there are minefields?" Star Captain Greer asked over the private comm circuit.

"If there are minefields, Star Captain, then we will clear them by running over them at speed."

"Sir?" The other man knew better than to question an order from his superior, but he was nevertheless able to infuse the respectful monosyllable with unspoken doubt. It was a useful skill for a soldier to have, and Darwin decided to honor it with an explanation.

"We can afford to lose a tank better than we can afford to lose time," he said. "The Highlanders are gathering, calling in their forces, setting up their defenses. Can you not smell it on the wind?"

"Sir." There was no direct agreement in that one-word answer, but no doubt or hesitation either—if the commander could smell it, the tone of voice implied, then that was enough.

Nicholas Darwin slammed his hand onto the armored ring around the Condor's top hatch.

"Forward," he said over the general circuit. "Leave the slower-moving vehicles behind to catch up with us. We are advancing. Maximum speed."

"What about the possibility of ambush, sir?" Greer asked over the command circuit.

Still on the general circuit, Darwin replied, "When we come into range of the enemy, they will be in range of us. All units, forward!"

With a sound like a rising whirlwind, the powerful hoverjets of the Condor tank raised it from the valley floor and impelled it into motion.

Behind it, the column advanced.

"I don't like it," Will Gordon said.

In company with Lexa McIntosh and Jock Gordon, he currently occupied a position in a hastily dug hole on the side of a scree slope. The three of them had been sent there in the small hours of the morning, after driving back along Highway 66 at top speed in order to rejoin the main body of the Highlander task force.

They had camouflaged their position as well as they could with branches and with tall grass, and had set up with their rifles looking across the valley to the west—the direction from which the Steel Wolves would soon be coming.

Now the morning sun shone down on their position through patchy clouds, warming Will's body after the chilly night, but failing to lift his spirits.

"It's too quiet," he continued. "Like something big came through and scared all the game away."

"I'm glad to hear that you don't like it," said Sergeant Donohue, approaching their position from the uphill side. He'd been inspecting the positions the ad hoc group had taken. "Battalion doesn't like not knowing what's out there, so they asked company. And company doesn't know and didn't know what was out there, and they didn't like that. So they called all the platoons to ask. And the platoons didn't know, so they asked the different squads if any of them had a clue as to what was out there. Nobody did. Unless you happen to know?"

Will shook his head. "Not a clue, Sergeant."

"Wonderful, Elliot," Sergeant Donohue said. "Because—since you and your pals did so well at playing find-the-Wolf last night—I'm tasking the three of you to go find out."

"You were saying?" Lexa said to Will under her breath. "Why couldn't you leave well enough alone?"

"Never tell a Sergeant that you don't have anything to do," Jock Gordon agreed. He shouldered his pack and picked up his rifle. "Radio silence, they said?"

"Yeah," Donohue said. "Get the word back without using your squawk boxes if you can. But if you're in a position where otherwise the Steel Wolves would reach us before the word did—then go ahead and use 'em. And if you're about to get overrun, use 'em. Anything else, mum's the word."

"Speaking of mums, is yours still rolling sailors?" Jock said, but he said it so quietly that the Sergeant didn't have to admit to hearing him. The three comrades picked up their weapons and headed off downslope and to the east.

"Any other bright ideas, Will?" Lexa asked after a few moments. "Seeing as you're so full of the spirit of helpfulness this morning."

"If we're going to watch for the Steel Wolves, then we're going to need a lookout spot," Will said. "And I think I know a place near here where we can do some looking out."

"Sounds good," Jock said. "Not too far, I hope? We've been awake and moving all of a day and all of a night, and now it looks like it's going to be all day again."

"Bitch, bitch, bitch," said Lexa.

"A bitching soldier is a happy soldier," Will said. "And if I don't miss my guess, we're going to have even more to be happy about before the morning's up."

42

Red Ledge Pass
Bloodstone Range of the Rockspire Mountains
Northwind
June, 3133; local summer

"Blocked?" Nicholas Darwin demanded of Scout Team Gamma over the tank radio. "What do you mean the road is blocked?"

"The Highlanders have used demolition gear to drop a cliff face across the road, Star Colonel," said the crackling, distance-attenuated voice of the leader of Scout Team Gamma. "Nothing on wheels or tracks will go through until we clear it."

"How long will that take?"

"Two hours at most. We have a MiningMech coming forward to deal with it."

Two hours. Darwin looked at the sun, climbing ever higher into the sky. Time was passing, inexorably. Time that he did not have. "Will hovercraft be able to pass?"

"Neg, Star Colonel. The rubble is too uneven and too steep."

"Then we will put the infantry over it," Darwin said. He keyed on the general circuit. "Anyone with jump jets, forward. We are wasting the Galaxy Commander's time."

After two hours of hard labor, the block was cleared. Darwin watched as the first of the Steel Wolves' wheeled vehicles made the narrow passage.

"Form up on the far side," he ordered.

Star Captain Greer commented, "We haven't heard from the infantry."

"In these mountains that's not surprising."

Will and Lexa and Jock lay against a ridge, looking west toward the mountains. A shoulder of hillside that moments before had been bare ground now crawled with figures in Steel Wolf uniforms and battle armor.

"That's them, isn't it?" Lexa asked. She took a sight with her laser rifle at one of the figures and shook her head regretfully. "Way out of range yet."

"Aye, that's them," Will said.

"I thought they had heavies with them," Jock said. "Are you sure we're looking at the main body?"

"This is the only way through," Will said. "Let's go back and tell the Sergeant what we saw. Maybe he'll let us have our old shelter back."

"Good plan," said Lexa. "I like it."

Jock nodded. "Let's go."

The three of them slid backward until the crest line concealed them, then stood and began to trot back to their own lines.

"We'll probably get shot at by our own people on the way in," Jock grumbled as they approached the encampment. "Everyone is that nervous."

"Pessimist," said Lexa.

Will ignored their byplay. He was still thinking about the enemy soldiers they had seen coming around the side of the mountain. "Who'd have thought the Steel Wolves would try this stunt with nothing but infantry?"

"Nothing but infantry?" Colonel Michael Griffin asked.

"That's the report," said Lieutenant Jones over the radio in his Joust tank. "And we have a fix on the location."

Part of the map in the *Koshi*'s cockpit display went solid red. The enemy weren't as far away as Griffin had hoped, but at least they were farther off than he had feared.

"Hold your fire until they're within half of nominal range," he ordered. "Then salvo-fire. Plaster the whole front."

"We don't have the ammunition to sustain that rate of fire, sir," Jones cautioned him.

"I know that," Griffin replied. "And you know that. But the Steel Wolves don't know that, and I want them to think that they've walked into a meat grinder and I'm turning the crank. When they get here, fire as if we were sitting on top of a whole ammunition dump. The only thing worse than running out of ammo is having the enemy think that we're low on bang juice."

"Still . . . nothing but infantry," Jones commented over his tank radio. "I wonder what that means? Could they be trying to draw us out?"

"Maybe," said Griffin.

At that moment, a whole armored infantry platoon carrying flamers came jump jetting out of the sky, and Griffin abruptly had his hands full. He jumped downslope to a position beside a stand of trees. The infantry platoon's flamers might heat him up enough to shut down the power plant—but not soon, not with a *Koshi*'s superior heat dissipation.

The *Koshi*'s exterior mikes picked up the sound of the guns on Jones's tank opening up. Griffin pitied the infantry that had tried to close assault his aide. He jumped again.

He was still in the air when the first shoulder-launched missile hit him. At least the 'Mech's gyros didn't tumble, although the missile's impact spun him around and turned his jump into a stumble-and-fall when he touched down.

"All circuits, go active," he ordered even as he brought his 'Mech back to its feet. "I want sensors up and radiating."

The area of blue mist on the cockpit map pushed outward as he complied with his own order. One look at the changed display was enough to reveal a map dotted with red spots, like a face with measles.

"Fire on targets of opportunity," Griffin said. "But do not advance. Hold in position, even if the enemy falls back."

If this was a trick, he thought, the Highlanders would not be taken in by it.

Then the world exploded around him—clods of earth flinging up, the stand of trees around him gone to splinters. Someone out there was sure carrying a lethal load for an infantry trooper. He started trotting up the line to where his aide's Joust was laying down a blanket of fire on the attackers.

A group of Steel Wolf regular infantry scrambled out of the way of Griffin's passage. They had to know, he thought as he watched them run, that the short-range missiles on the arms of his *Koshi* were too valuable to waste on unarmored infantry when there soon might be more dangerous prey available—but the arms and legs of twenty-five tons of forged ferro-fiber doing seventy-five kilometers per hour were still terrifying and deadly to a man armored with nothing thicker than his shirt.

43

Eastern Slopes of the Bloodstone Range
Rockspire Mountains, Northwind
June, 3133; local summer

Nicholas Darwin saw the smoke before he could hear the sounds of combat. "Has any of the infantry reported?" he asked.

"We are getting scattered reports," the communications operator said. "There is at least one 'Mech."

"Class?"

"Reports range from light to heavy."

"What kind of resistance?" Darwin asked. "And where is the smoke line on the map?"

"Resistance is definitely heavy," said the Condor's sensor operator, and indicated an area on the tank's battlefield display. "The smoke line is here."

"Very well." Darwin opened up the general command circuit. "Draw up a skirmish line, and on my command, volley fire, blind, onto the smoke line. Then advance, taking all targets under fire as they appear."

Whoever was holding the pass for the Highlanders was good, Darwin reflected as he gave his orders. Now that he had seen the area at the mouth of the pass, he had to admit that he would have chosen the same site himself for a defensive line. So either the enemy commander was very clever, or he and Darwin were both equally stupid. Now that battle was engaged, there was no way to tell except by fighting it out.

"Now," Darwin said. "Volley."

With a whoosh and a vapor trail that rolled white across the lines, the missile launchers fired.

"Now—" he started to say again.

"Incoming, sir!"

From the area ahead that had just been their target, a line of arced vapor trails were approaching. Then flowers of fire began to blossom in the air.

"Short-range antitactical defenses up," Darwin ordered. "Wolves, we are moving forward. Our armor will take anything that does not break the heart."

The valley had been pretty.

Then the explosions came.

"Our right flank reports heavy pressure," Lieutenant Jones said, "and they're low on ammo."

"I'll be up there," Griffin said. "Get a report from the SP guns while I'm away."

Then he was running, jumping, running again, to the right flank.

He passed dead men and broken machines, but did not stop. Then he was at a scree slope, and the traces of fire, pulses of energy in the air, the dazzle of lasers, and the crump of ordinary kinetic shells, filled his sensors and his inputs.

A Condor hovertank showed up to his left on the cockpit display. He twisted, sent a battery of SRMs at the Condor, then jumped before it could target him. On external comms, he said, "Highlanders! Rally here."

Infantry emerged from foxholes and from covering terrain. He couldn't see their expressions from his position high up in the *Koshi*'s towering frame, but judging from their overall body language and the quickness of their response, they were scared but resolute. Not bad for new, mostly unblooded troops, he thought—and the ones who lived through today would be new and unblooded no longer.

"We're going to back slowly to the center," he said, "and then make a fighting retreat. With me."

As he spoke, he directed another battery of missiles, this one from his right arm, at a sensor trace near the edge of his maximum range. "I'll cover you, and hold here long enough for you to get away."

The troops shifted back, one of them, a tall man, raising his Gauss rifle and firing from the shoulder at something Griffin couldn't see even as he set out toward the rear.

"Good idea," said Griffin. "The best defense is a good offense."

He started running toward the attacking Wolves. Time now to confuse them. Make them turn to one side or another. Keep them away from Tara. He checked the time readout on the cockpit chronometer as he ran.

The Countess had asked for twelve hours more. So far he'd given her eight. He could do another four . . . the readouts for ammo said that his left arm was down to what was in the pods, then no more reloads. Heat wasn't bad, though.

A Schmitt tank lay in his path ahead. Something the Steel Wolves had brought along for fighting in the streets of Tara, no doubt. Well, it wouldn't get there.

Griffin jumped, and aimed for the turret of the tank. His impact with both feet blew two of the tires on the vehicle's left side. That would slow them down. He rolled off toward the back of the Schmitt, avoiding its flamers. He was too close for the long-range missiles to lock on to him. And unlike the infantry, he could ignore its machine guns.

A set of shocks up his right arm and across his back reminded him of the Schmitt's autocannon. While the tank might be immobilized it could still reach out and hit him.

He dodged around a rock wall, and came face-to-face with an SM1 Tank Destroyer. He sent a battery of missiles into its turret. He turned before he could see what damage he'd inflicted, saw the crippled Schmitt, and sent two more missiles into the tank's rear armor. The hatches blew off and a smoke ring of oily black shot from the top. That one, at least, wouldn't be repaired.

Griffin headed back for the Highlander lines at a run.

"Retreat, fall back," he said over the command circuit. "Drop back to rally point one. Set up hasty defenses. Every man—take out one Steel Wolf and we'll call this day ours."

He looked at the countdown clock. Hold out three hours and forty minutes more. He would. He had to.

It was the damned *Koshi,* Darwin thought.

He had seen the Highlanders falling back and had rejoiced, knowing that when they abandoned the fight the way would lie clear for the main body of the Steel Wolves to pour through the mountain pass and out onto the rolling plains north of Tara. But the seeming rout had not lasted; the fleeing infantry had halted and reformed their battle line and were once again standing fast.

The MechWarrior in the *Koshi* was everywhere along the line, courting heat overload with reckless abandon, using his jump jets and his hundred-plus kilometers per hour maximum speed to take himself to wherever the fighting was thickest and the infantry needed the most support. He was the heart and soul of the Highlanders' resistance, and Darwin knew better than to hope that the *Koshi*'s superior heat efficiency would fail in time to give the Steel Wolves any help.

He keyed on the command communications circuit. "Star Captain Greer. Take whatever forces you need, and kill me that *Koshi*."

The Highlanders' new defenses were holding, but Michael Griffin knew better than to expect that his own luck would do likewise. The *Koshi* had to be one of the most tempting targets on the entire battlefield, and the enemy commander had to have guessed that the Highlanders' MechWarrior was the leader responsible for their deceptive rout and fresh resistance.

The massive volley of short-range missiles that came down on his position was not unexpected—the level of overkill was almost a compliment if you looked at it the right way—but the simultaneous disabling hits to the *Koshi*'s left leg, right shoulder, and torso were more at once than the 'Mech's internal stabilizing systems could take. The cockpit instruments blinked and faded, the footpedals and pressure controls ceased responding, and the *Koshi*'s entire massive body swayed and fell.

The command couch took the greater part of the impact, leaving Griffin mostly unhurt, though he would have bruises later and perhaps a broken bone or two—if he lived long enough to count them, he thought, struggling with the couch straps. The cockpit displays were all either down or wavering erratically, but what he could see of the field outside with his own eyes didn't look promising.

Missiles hadn't been good enough for the enemy commander, when it came time to take out the *Koshi*. The Wolves had sent in a follow-up crew of Elemental infantry to make certain the MechWarrior inside didn't get out alive.

Griffin reached for the slug pistol he kept in the *Koshi*'s cockpit for occasions such as this. He couldn't do much damage with it, not to genetically enhanced warriors in powered armor, but at least he could go down fighting.

Then the bright beam of a laser cut across his field of vision, and he heard, dimly through the *Koshi*'s metal hull, the ripping noise of machine gun fire and the crunching sound of a long-range missile impact. The Elementals scattered and backed off, and a moment later Griffin heard the sound of hammering on the *Koshi*'s cockpit hatch.

"Colonel Griffin, sir!" a voice was shouting. "Lieutenant Jones says to get your ass out of there and into his Joust before the gorillas pull together and come back to try again!"

Griffin checked the cockpit chronometer—amazingly enough, it still ran. Fifteen minutes left, he thought; close enough. We've done it.

The infantry had held the line.

PART FIVE

Northwind, Early Summer 3133
The Battle for Tara

44

The plains north of Tara
Northwind
June, 3133; local summer

Rain had been spitting down in a desultory fashion ever since the middle of the morning; now the clouds were growing thicker and the wind was picking up. Will Elliot, along with Jock Gordon and Lexa McIntosh, paused by the side of the road to take a breath before moving on.

Will hadn't slept in a day and a half now—and the half day most recent had been full of fire and speed, shooting and running, hitching rides along with Jock and Lexa on any vehicle they could find after the scout car assigned to the three-person team developed too much yaw from a near miss. The Highlanders' holding action at the mouth of Red Ledge Pass had turned into a long retreat, a retreat prevented from becoming a rout only by Colonel Griffin's solid example and careful orders. At one point a rumor had flown through the Highlander ranks that Griffin's 'Mech was down and the Colonel was dead, but the sound of his voice giving orders over the command circuit soon put that idea to rest.

"When do you think it'll be over?" Lexa asked wearily. She was leaning against a boulder and working the tangles out of her dark hair with a pocket comb. What she hoped to accomplish that way Will couldn't imagine, since she was as covered with sweat and ground-in dirt as her two comrades, but since it seemed to make her feel better he forbore to comment.

"It'll stop when we're dead or they are," he told her instead. He checked the power pack in his Gauss rifle. Close to redline—and he only had one more replacement in the cargo pocket of his fatigues. "Damn—where's Central Supply when you really need them?"

"They got lost, same as everyone else," Jock said.

"I'm not lost," Will said. "Tara's up ahead a day or so, depending on how fast we run. Closer, if we get a ride."

"There's no safety if we run."

"If you wanted safety," Will said, "you should have stayed home on the farm. Let's see if the Sergeant has any orders for us. If he doesn't, maybe we can make our own fun."

"Promises, promises," Lexa said, sliding the comb back into her pocket and pushing away from the boulder.

"If you ask me, finding a place to sleep sounds like a fine idea," Jock said.

Will shook his head. "Only if I wanted to wake up under the foot of a Steel Wolf 'Mech. Now—"

"We've got trucks." A man from the Northwind Fusiliers came up the road at a half run. "Radio silence, everyone. Trucks. We're falling back. Rally point is at grid position nine–one–forty–three. Pass it on to everyone you see."

He continued running down the road and out of sight. The three comrades looked at each other.

"So what's that all about?" Lexa asked.

"I don't take orders from a Corporal in the Fuzies," Jock said.

"All right, people," Sergeant Donohue said, appearing suddenly out of the underbrush on the shoulder of the road. Unlike almost everybody else Will had seen in the past few hours, the Sergeant didn't look either tired or rumpled, and Will wondered, not for the first time, if the man had his uniform tattooed onto his body. "Why aren't you saddling up? We've got some trucks to catch."

"What's the word, Sarge?" Lexa asked. "Where are we going?"

"If I knew, I'd tell you." The Sergeant looked around. "Where's Corporal McCloud?"

"Last I saw, up at the observation post," Will replied.

"Right. On your way." The Sergeant faded back into the underbrush.

"Sounds like we have our orders," Jock said.

"Let's move, then," Will said. He slung his pack onto his shoulders, picked up his rifle, and headed off at a trot for the staging area, with Lexa and Jock running beside him.

At the staging area, there were indeed trucks waiting, and hot food too, trucked in. A medical corpsman had an aid station going under a tent flap rigged from the side of one truck; a chaplain was holding services at another truck, standing up in the truck bed so that he looked down on his makeshift congregation.

"Either of you need any of that?" Lexa asked.

"What I want is some of my mum's homemade berry tart," Will said. "That'd make me right. But since what we have is army meat and army bread—"

"—which comes from no known animal or plant—" Jock chimed in.

"—every day's a holiday and every meal's a feast," Lexa finished. "Here comes an officer; maybe he knows something."

The officer in question—a Major with a bullhorn—took the chaplain's place on the back of the truck as soon as the service was finished.

"Listen up, people," he said. "I want everyone with anti-armor weapons and ammo up in the lead vehicle." He gestured to his left. "If you have antiarmor, move up there now. If there are more than will fit, take the second truck, and the third, and so on." He paused. "If you have anti-air weapons, I want you in the middle truck, that's truck side number six–zero–four, right here where I'm standing. Move there now." He paused again. "Everyone with unused demolition charges or special heavy weapons—heavy machine guns, rocket launchers, mortars, move to the rear of the convoy. Last truck, people. Fill in forward from there. Move now."

The Major paused yet again while Will chewed on the army bread. It wasn't fresh, but it wasn't tasty either. On the other hand, it had a shelf life measured in decades, and contained the minimum daily requirement of almost everything except fun.

The Major's voice came over the bullhorn one more time. "Everyone else, pick a place on one of the remaining vehicles. Go there. The column is pulling out in five minutes."

The truck to the left of the middle vehicle was empty. Will nodded in that direction and said to the others, "You heard the man—let's get on board while there are still seats. Maybe someone on the truck can tell us where we're going."

"If you ask me," said Lexa with pessimistic relish, "this is all an absolute disaster, and the only place we're going is straight to hell."

"Why do you say that?" Will asked as he climbed over the tailboards. Bench seats lined the sides of the truck. He headed forward to where the back of the cab would provide some shelter against what looked like was turning into a vile evening.

"We're advancing to the rear in glorious victory against a foe that is routing forward in utter disorder," Lexa said. "At this rate the Steel Wolves are going to be in the capital by daybreak. No one knows what we have or where we are—including our own side. Our units are all broken up. If I was calling this 'every man for himself' how wrong would I be?"

"Not very," said Jock. "It looks like it's the three of us against the world."

"Then the world had better watch out," Will said.

The truck soon filled up with more men and women, some with full kit, others carrying nothing more than a rifle and a satchel of spare charges. In fewer than the promised five minutes the humming note of the truck's engine lowered and they lurched forward. The spot against the back wall of the cab proved to be a good one. Will, Lexa, and Jock only got wet on one side when the clouds opened and the rain poured down half an hour into their trip.

45

Plains north of Tara; the Fort
Northwind
June, 3133; local summer

Nicholas Darwin sat atop his Condor tank, relishing the cool evening air after a day spent in the rank, stuffy confines of the tank's interior, and listening to the communications chatter among the Warriors of his command. A light mist drifted down from the cloudy sky, cooling his skin, and the faint whiff of ozone from the Condor's main gun told of a battle won. Anastasia Kerensky would be pleased.

"Resistance is crumbling, Star Colonel," Star Captain Greer reported over the command circuit. "We are taking light small-arms fire only. No heavy guns. No sign of enemy 'Mechs."

"Very well," Darwin said. "Exit the valley."

He turned to the communications operator in the Condor tank. "Send a signal to Galaxy Commander Anastasia Kerensky: Route secure. Preparing to advance."

"As you command, Star Colonel," said Greer, and the communications officer said, "Message sent."

Darwin swung back down into the body of the tank. Time to start moving again.

"Once we are on the plain," he ordered, "take formation. Skirmishers forward, hovercraft on the flanks. I do not desire surprises."

"What about the Highlanders, Star Colonel?" asked Greer.

"The Highland line is broken," Darwin said. "Bypass the ones who will not surrender. We can mop them up later."

"Yes, sir."

Ezekiel Crow closed the office door behind him and leaned back against it with a heavy sigh of exhaustion. The departure from his usual unbending posture spoke volumes to Tara Campbell about the depths of his fatigue. She herself was propped half standing, half sitting on the edge of the room's heavy wooden desk. One more minute spent standing tall and unwavering, she was convinced, would have had her toppling like a felled tree.

Tara and Crow had met in the Prefect's small office in the depths of the Fort in order to go over the latest battlefield intelligence reports. By unspoken agreement, they had left the Combat Information Center in order to have that conversation in private. There was no point in making other people into unwilling eavesdroppers on a discussion that might damage their morale.

Tara still had her freshly updated data pad in her hand; the Paladin made a weary gesture in its general direction.

"What do we have by way of reinforcements?" he asked.

"Nothing we didn't have last night," she said. "Mostly those Tyson and Varney retrofit 'Mechs. But they are all in the city now and moving west."

He nodded slowly, not looking at her, his gaze fixed on something out beyond the toes of his boots. "It's enough to let us set up a line half a day out. If we hold, we can at least give the civilians time to evacuate."

"What do you mean—'evacuate'?" she demanded. "Do you honestly think we're so outclassed it'll come to that?"

"I don't want anyone to come home to find their parents shot in their beds," he replied, tight-lipped. He looked up at her then, his blue eyes intent and blazing. "Yes, move them out. All the available transport that isn't needed for the fighting—that isn't crucial to the fighting—should be ferrying noncombatants away."

"Are you sure?" she asked.

"If you want to sleep at night afterward."

"I'll give the order."

He looked back down at his feet, as if embarrassed by his own sudden vehemence. "Thank you," he said quietly.

"It's all right," she said. There was an awkward silence. Then Tara cleared her throat and consulted the data pad again. "The aerospace fighter wing out of Halidon will be overhead by dawn if they can make it through at all. The weather doesn't look good."

"Radick and his Steel Wolves aren't going to give us until dawn," Crow said. "After fighting their way through the pass, they'll be too hungry for that."

"We'll do what we can." Tara made some adjustments to the data pad and called up a rough, diagrammatic map. She passed the data pad over to Crow, saying, "I know a good place to do this. Halfway from here to the mountains. Look—I've got it marked."

Crow took the data pad and glanced over the contents of the display. "What's the ground like?"

"Low rolling hills, mostly," Tara said. "We can draw up our forces along this north-south ridgeline, with the tanks hull-down just over the crest. There's a stream along the bottom of the ridge that might slow down some of their tracked vehicles."

"Speaking of slowing them down . . . has there been any new word from Colonel Griffin?"

She shook her head. "You were there for the last one."

"Then we have to assume that he has fallen, and make our plans accordingly."

"He promised me the time," she said. "He'll deliver it whether he's fallen or not."

She forced herself to stand up straight and pull her shoulders back, in what she hoped was a convincing facsimile of a ready-for-anything posture. "And if his time isn't going to be wasted, you and I need to get into our 'Mechs and start the army moving."

46

Plains north of Tara
Northwind
June, 3133; local summer

The approaching storm brought darkness unnaturally early to the plains north of the capital. Lowering clouds obscured the sunset and hid the twilight stars from view. Shifting, unpredictable gusts of wind disturbed the still air at irregular intervals, throwing up dust and leaves into miniature whirlwinds that swirled briefly in the headlight glare of passing vehicles, then fell apart.

The Northwind Highlanders had set up their advance command post in the gymnasium of an abandoned consolidated secondary school. The small farming and grazing communities of the plain had emptied out upon hearing that the

Wolves were in the northern pass; the capital was packed with refugees.

If we fail now, Tara Campbell thought with an inward shiver, the whole city is vulnerable. And we cannot evacuate everyone in time. No matter how hard we try.

She said nothing aloud, however; Michael Griffin and Ezekiel Crow, who stood with her at the communications center—a fine name for what was in reality no more than a collection of modular consoles set up at one end of the gymnasium underneath the game clock and the scoreboard—both understood the situation without having her betray her own nerves by mentioning it. And Crow, at least, who knew firsthand what could happen when enemy troops ran wild in a city, would not appreciate having those memories stirred up without need.

One of the consoles beeped and spat out a printed sheet. Michael Griffin retrieved the paper and scanned it, frowning. Griffin had sustained several broken ribs in the last minutes of the battle for Red Ledge Pass, and his *Koshi* would lie on the field of battle until one side or the other won the war and brought the crippled 'Mech in for repairs, but he had refused to leave the front lines.

"Meteorology reports bad weather coming," Griffin said.

"We didn't need Meteorology to tell us that," Tara said. "Do they have anything more specific?"

"There's a major storm system coming up

from the southeast; it should hit the local area around dawn. The forecast calls for high winds, heavy rain, thunderstorm activity, and localized flooding."

Ezekiel Crow said, "That's not good weather for 'Mechs and armor."

"That's not good weather for anything," Tara said. She tugged distractedly at a strand of her yellow hair—when she was a little girl, she'd believed that the harder she pulled, the better she thought, and in times of stress her fingers believed it still—and came to a decision. She turned to the communications tech on duty and said, "Broadcast a message on the open channel. Tell Prefect Kal Radick that we want to parley."

Griffin stared at her. "We want what?"

The Colonel was visibly taken aback by her proposal, as was Ezekiel Crow. Tara made haste to reassure them.

"I want to propose a temporary ceasefire until the storm system passes. That's all. Fighting conditions aside, we can always use the extra time."

The signal went out, and within minutes, Tara and Ezekiel Crow were in a Fox armored car, heading out for the designated meeting place—a set of map coordinates in the midst of open ground not held by either army. The drive from their temporary headquarters took close to an hour, even at speed. Nobody wanted the leader of the Steel Wolves any closer to the Highlander lines than that, even for a parley, and by the time they reached the gridposition, it was full night. They exited the Fox, leaving all the vehicle's lights on and blinking as per the arranged signal, and waited.

The Wolves were prompt. Only a few minutes passed before Tara saw a vehicle approaching from the north—another Fox armored car, this one bearing Steel Wolf insignia. The Fox came to a halt a few meters off and two people got out, a woman and a man. They drew closer—and Tara repressed shock, keeping her face still with effort.

The man was not Kal Radick. Tara knew enough about Steel Wolf gear and uniforms to see that he wore the insignia of a Star Colonel, but not that of a MechWarrior. The woman, though—with her dangerous good looks, nobody was ever going to call that one the Angel of Anyplace, or try to make her over into a recruiting-poster darling, and for an instant Tara felt a wash of pure, irrational envy. Things in the Steel Wolves had clearly changed faster than the Highlanders' intelligence reports could keep up with, because the woman was the one in charge.

"Galaxy Commander," Tara said. It was a good thing, she thought, that she'd trained in diplomacy from toddlerhood on up. She could keep a calm face and a polite voice no matter what the circumstances. "Am I to infer, then, that Kal Radick no longer leads the Steel Wolves?"

The woman gave a curt nod. "You are. I am Anastasia Kerensky."

Hell, thought Tara. A Kerensky. Stay calm,

and don't ask what happened to Radick. She probably cut his throat and ate him boiled for breakfast.

Her answering nod was as brief as Kerensky's had been; perhaps even a fraction briefer. When she spoke, her voice was cool and steady. "I am Tara Campbell, Countess of Northwind and Prefect of Prefecture III. My companion is Paladin Ezekiel Crow."

Crow had donned plain civilian attire for the parley, thus avoiding rank insignia entirely—a tactful move, ensuring that he did not undercut Tara's authority as Countess and Prefect. Polite as ever, he bowed and said, "Galaxy Commander Kerensky."

She nodded. "Paladin."

Tara looked at Anastasia Kerensky's male companion, the Star Colonel. Her expectant expression did no good; Kerensky didn't provide any identification. If the man resented the omission, it didn't show.

Politeness, Tara reminded herself. Ever politeness. "I asked for this parley, Galaxy Commander, in order to give you and yours one last chance to leave Northwind in peace."

She'd expected a refusal. The offer was a standard opening, like the Ruy Lopez in chess. She hadn't expected outright contemptuous laughter, in which the Star Colonel joined.

"Why should we leave?" Kerensky demanded. "We have taken out your air support, we have pushed through the mountains, we are poised even now to capture your capital. Northwind is as good as ours."

Tara kept her face calm, and put on what she privately thought of as Polite Smile Number Twenty-three, the one which implied that the speaker had made a gross public gaffe but couldn't be expected to know any better. The Kerensky woman's lips tightened; she'd obviously spent enough time outside the Clan enclaves that she could recognize the expression and know what it meant.

Tara said, "Don't go claiming Northwind just yet, Galaxy Commander." The Clans didn't like casual language and contractions; the imprecision irritated them. Irritating Anastasia Kerensky seemed like a good idea just now, or at least an enjoyable one. "There's the small matter of a battle that we've got to deal with first."

Kerensky's hand—the splinted and bandaged one—twitched slightly, as if at another time and place she'd be pounding a table. Tara noted the motion. It was nice to know that impatience was an issue here.

"Then by all means," Kerensky said, "let us fight the battle and be done with it."

"Of course . . . but perhaps not today." Before Kerensky could draw breath for an indignant reply, Tara said, "Have you taken a look at the sky lately? There's the mother and father of a storm system rolling in, and it's not going to let up until tomorrow afternoon at least. If you aren't going to do the sensible thing and leave Northwind, then I'd like to propose a thirty-six-hour ceasefire to let both sides wait out the bad weather."

Kerensky's lip curled. "Afraid to fight in the rain, Countess?"

"Not crazy enough to think I'm proof against the lightning, Galaxy Commander."

"And I am not crazy enough to let talk of bad weather scare me into losing an advantage. No ceasefire, Countess."

"In that case, Galaxy Commander, we fight, and let the rain fall on both of us equally—on the just and on the unjust, as it were." Tara smiled again, because it seemed to annoy Kerensky when she did so. "Are you sure you don't want to take my offer? I do have the advantage of knowing what the summer weather around here can be like."

"No," said Kerensky, thin-lipped. "No ceasefire."

Tara glanced over at Ezekiel Crow. They had discussed this bit in the Fox on the drive out to the rendezvous point, and now it was his turn to speak.

"The Prefect has warned you off of Northwind explicitly," he said, "and has three times offered you an honorable avenue of escape or delay—offers that have three times been refused." His lean dark face was somber, his eyes grave. "As a Paladin of the Sphere, I must warn you: You are officially considered to be in active rebellion against the Republic, and must expect to be dealt with accordingly."

Once again, Anastasia Kerensky laughed. "If there were any honor in it, only your heads would return to your Highland rabble. This parley is over."

She turned and strode back to her waiting vehicle. Over her shoulder, she said, "Star Colonel."

The man who had come with her moved to follow, but not before raising a handheld radio to his lips. "Advance column, this is Darwin. Weapons free. Forward."

47

Plains north of Tara
Northwind
June, 3133; local summer

The truck carrying Will Elliot and his friends lurched to a stop in the rain-filled dawn. Will had fallen asleep sitting up in the corner behind the cab, and the abrupt cessation of the truck's motion brought him awake with a start, grabbing for his Gauss rifle with one hand and his pack with the other. Somebody else had fallen asleep leaning on his shoulder; from the size and feel, it was probably Lexa McIntosh.

And both of us too tired to appreciate the experience, Will thought.

"Right, then," a Sergeant's voice shouted. Will didn't recognize the speaker, but only a Sergeant could yell like that. "Out of the trucks. Find your units."

"Here we go," Lexa said, pushing herself

away from Will's shoulder. "Now we get to add muddy to wet."

The three unloaded from their truck. The falling rain kept the sky dark, almost black, in spite of the early morning hour, with no visibility beyond the reach of the truck's headlights. Will heard the rushing of a stream nearby, and checked his compass.

"We've come a long way," he said, "but we've got unfriendlies coming up behind us. The Wolves are heading straight for Tara, and we're standing right in their path."

Out in the dark, a Sergeant was shouting again. "Set up, form up!"

Will and the other Highlanders from the truck drew up in a ragged formation. The Sergeant this time turned out to be Master Sergeant Murray, the same man who had sent Will and his friends on their reconnaissance mission the day before. Murray paused on his way down the line to give the three of them a long look before continuing on.

"Gather round, children," Murray said, after he had reached the end of the line.

They gathered.

"Well, lads and lasses," Murray continued, "here's the word from company: This is where the Highlanders save Northwind. But on the off chance that we don't save it, if you get separated from your unit make your best way to Carcross. That's in the hills, off any of the main highways the Wolves are likely to be using. And hold on, hold out, right here, as long as you can."

"That's it, Sergeant?" Lexa asked. "That doesn't sound like much of a plan."

"That's what company had for us," Murray said. "But here's what I have for you. You're infantry. Don't try to mix it up with tanks or 'Mechs. They'll eat you for breakfast and go looking for more. Your job is enemy infantry, and their skins aren't any thicker than yours. Keep them off the 'Mechs and the tanks. If one of our units gets in trouble, support it. If one of their units gets in trouble, use your can openers.

"If you can take an enemy 'Mech—and I don't want anyone here to go looking, because 'hero' is a name people give to dead men—but if you *can* take an enemy 'Mech, take it intact. Those things are valuable and we're going to need every one of them we can get our hands on. If you can get their MechWarrior out alive, even better. Those people have information that our side needs, and they have high value in hostage exchanges.

"If you have to destroy a 'Mech, though, do it. Better a burned-out hulk on the battlefield with a crispy at the controls than an active opponent.

"Now, form groups of four, get a location to the west of the stream, and dig in."

"How long do we have, Sarge?" Jock Gordon asked.

A long, lancing arc of fire sprang overhead, from away in the west. It passed above them low and fast, heading east, and an explosion bloomed behind the ridge line.

"They're here right now. Places, everyone. Remember, stay loose, and no heroes."

* * *

It was going to be a long, hot morning in spite of the cold wind and the rain outside.

Anastasia Kerensky had dressed down for the battle, wearing nothing but a pair of shorts under her MechWarrior's cooling vest. She did not expect to leave the cockpit of her 'Mech until she had driven the Highlanders out of Tara.

The *Ryoken II*'s massive head swayed as she looked north and south along the lines of troops and tanks that were the striking force of the Steel Wolves, and to the east at the Highlanders arrayed against her. Her 'Mech's cockpit display showed the location and status of all friendly units, including those not directly visible, with markers indicating presumed enemy locations as the intelligence came in.

The Highlanders have a thin line, she thought, and a brittle one. Crack it at any place and it will shatter, leaving the road to Tara open.

"On my command," she said. "Artillery. Find targets. Lock on. Fire." And again, "Artillery. Fire." And a third time, "Artillery. Fire."

Then, "On my command. Long-range missiles. Fire."

An overarching curtain of fire, torn and obscured by rain and wind, spread out over the opposing troops in response to her words. Ahead of her, the artillery shells were already detonating, the light of their explosions refracted in the lashing rain.

The rain would be hell on the infantry, Wolf and Highlander alike, but in her 'Mech Anastasia was dry. And the rain would help cool her *Ryoken II* even as it strode forward.

"Stay close," she ordered her troops. "Hovercraft, find the ends of their lines. Then swing around behind. Envelop them. I want attacks from the rear. I want attacks wherever you can find them. Forward, guide on me!"

She set the *Ryoken II* in motion toward the enemy lines, reveling Tassa Kay–like in the knowledge that she was about to do something which few in the Inner Sphere could do better. She was a Kerensky, and for those of her Bloodname, fighting in a BattleMech went gene-code deep. The 'Mech's skeleton was her skeleton, its armored skin, her skin. After a lifetime's practice, she needed no more thought to guide seventy-five tons of deadly metal than she needed to walk in boots and leather through the dark streets of Tigress or Dieron or Achernar.

"Galaxy Commander." The words sounded in her ear. "We are picking up a signal from the Northwind troops. They have it on all frequencies."

"Patch it through," she said. Now a smattering of fire was coming her way. Ahead, a tank destroyer behind a camouflage net spouted fire. She targeted it, without pausing to calculate, and sent a Streak in its direction. They would have to move or die.

A babble of rising and falling voices sounded over the cockpit's speakers.

"What is that?" Anastasia demanded.

"The Highlanders' signal, Galaxy Commander. They are singing."

Now that she was listening, she could make out words in the babble. " . . . *if you've never been laid on a Saturday night, you've never been laid at all!"*

"So they are," she said. "And badly." Though Tassa Kay remembered that chorus very well, and a Highlander on a boring DropShip transit who had claimed that the song had over five-hundred and fifty-six verses, though he himself could only recall forty-two of them.

He had been wrong. Tassa Kay had counted them one night, and he knew forty-seven, at least when he was drunk. Anastasia wondered if he was out there singing again today.

"The Highlanders are making their location known for us," she said. "Target them."

Beside her, a Demon tank stopped abruptly, lurching sidewise on melted and deflating tires as the ammo in its rotary autocannon arced and sparked. The Demon's hatch sprang open and its crew ran for cover—any second now, the tank's flamers would catch, and anyone left inside would be caught in the fireball. Anastasia traced back the probable trajectory of the barrage of missiles that had taken out the tank, and put a burst of pulse particles onto the location.

Forward, she thought. Do not outrun the troops, but lead them. The Highlanders have nothing, no hope of resistance, or they would not have been seeking delay.

A line of fire stitched up the *Ryoken II*'s leg, chewing at the surface layers of metal and myomer—an autocannon, tracking and ranging her. She spun toward the enemy and engaged the *Ryoken II*'s jump jets, in order to ruin the autocannon's firing solution.

Hitting the ground running, she sprinted toward the autocannon emplacement—past lasers to left and right, their light scattered by the rain but still burning through; past the mud . . . no, *into* the mud that was churning up. She was wading in mud. They'd drawn her into a bog.

She deployed the *Ryoken II*'s jump jets again, desperately seeking higher ground. Resistance as strong as this could not go on forever. The Highlanders were expending troops at a reckless rate.

"Star Colonel Darwin!" she demanded over the command circuit. "Darwin, report!"

"We are taking heavy fire," came the reply. "And there is a 'Mech over here . . . we have not made the ID yet. But we know it is fast, and the engineer says that it must have hell's own power plant . . . coordinates twelve-thirty-five-one."

"I am on my way," Anastasia said. A 'Mech like that had to belong to the Paladin. "If we are in open rebellion against The Republic, then so be it. Paladins will just have to take their chances."

48

Plains north of Tara
Northwind
June, 3133; local summer

"That's something you don't see every day," murmured Lexa McIntosh in Will's ear.

The two of them were sharing a hastily dug foxhole that threatened to fill up with rain before many more hours had passed. The drizzle that had come down intermittently all night was now a steady driving downpour, lashed into sideways sheets by the driving wind. Visibility wasn't much better than it had been during the night, except when the flashes of lightning lit up the open, rolling landscape.

"What is it?" Will asked.

"One—no, make that three—'Mechs. Crossing the ridge line."

"I don't see them."

"Wait for the next lightning flash . . . there."

Will squinted out through the rain. Yes, she was right. Three dark, lumbering shapes were moving out onto the battlefield and toward the Highlander lines.

"Identification," he said. "We need identification."

Lexa fumbled in the cargo pocket of her fatigue trousers and pulled out a waterproof flip chart of silhouettes. "Give me a moment to look 'em up, all right?"

"You mean you don't have them all memorized yet?"

Lexa sneered. "I don't see *you* calling out their marks and mods either."

Will looked over her shoulder as she riffled through the pages of the chart, then looked back toward the Steel Wolf lines. "These look like ForestryMechs," he said. "Maybe a MiningMech. Look at that big-ass saw."

"Not too dangerous, then," Lexa said.

"That's like saying a rabid bulldog isn't too dangerous just because it isn't a rabid lion," Will said. "And there's no telling what some of those retrofit jobs might have bolted on them. We ought to report them in."

Tara Campbell, in the cockpit of her *Hatchetman* BattleMech, held her position in the center of the Highlanders' battle line. Her work here would be command and control—and protecting the center of the line against the tanks, heavy artillery, and 'Mechs that Anastasia Kerensky would undoubtedly send against them. Meanwhile, Ezekiel Crow, in his lighter, faster

Blade, would be roving the battle from hot spot to hot spot, applying force and speed quickly where it was most needed.

A volley of smoke cylinders from the Highlander artillery discharged their white puffs of smoke in front of the battle line. The smoke was not as effective in the rain and wind as it would have been on a fair-weather battlefield, but every obscuring wisp was a small added advantage for the defenders, increasing the fog of war and making their numbers harder to guess and to target.

"Report," she said to the command talker over the *Hatchetman*'s comms. "I want the position of the nearest enemy 'Mechs."

"Word just in puts three Industrials out by gridposit twenty-one-twenty-three-eight," the command talker said.

She checked her cockpit map display. Gridposit 21–23–8 was close enough to be a direct threat to the center of the Northwind line. It looked like Anastasia Kerensky wasn't intending to do things the slow and careful way.

"Put a tank with medium-range missiles onto them," Tara ordered by way of the command talker. "I'll be along shortly."

She brought the *Hatchetman* striding out through the Highlander lines, heading for 21–23–8 at a steady, moderate pace. No need to build up too much heat in the opening of what promised to be a brisk and energetic dance. As she went, she looked about for the IndustrialMechs—and there they were, a trio of dark shapes looming up out of the fog and rain, ugly blocky things that lacked the clean, designed-to-kill lines of a true BattleMech. Nevertheless, the Schmitt tank engaging them was outclassed and clearly knew it, though it pressed its attack boldly, dashing in close to fire a volley and retreating rapidly out of range.

"These are mine," she said to the tank. "Get clear."

The Schmitt pulled away through the rain at top speed, waves of muddy water flying up from under its wheels as it ran. Lightning flashed overhead, and thunder rumbled as Tara Campbell engaged her prey.

Ezekiel Crow was hunting. The *Blade* BattleMech strode quickly through the fray, not pausing to expend its ammo on lesser targets than other 'Mechs. An all-day slugging match would not help the people of Tara. Even with all of the region's noncombatant public services put to work in the evacuation, no army could buy enough time for everyone in the city to reach safety. If the Highlander line broke—or even if the Highlanders did not break, but stood and died to the last man and the last woman—when the battle-maddened Steel Wolves poured into the streets of the capital, buildings would burn and people would die.

The only sure salvation lay in forcing the Wolves to retreat. And for that, he needed to engage the modified *Ryoken II* that battlefield intelligence reported as the mount of Anastasia Kerensky. Engage it, and kill it. Without their leader, the Steel Wolves would turn and run like the dogs they at heart remained.

"Do you have a location yet on the Wolves' commander?" he asked the command talker over the *Blade*'s cockpit comms.

"We're showing a big mass of iron five klicks on your left flank, at about the right speed constraints. That could be her."

"I'm going over to take a look." Crow moved from a trot to a run.

"Who is it rides the *Blade*?" Anastasia Kerensky demanded of the Steel Wolves' battlefield intelligence officer. "And who the *Hatchetman*?"

She could see both of the 'Mechs from where she was advancing toward the Highlander lines in her *Ryoken II*. The *Hatchetman* loomed over the infantry in the Northwind center—a hunch-shouldered, broad-chested brute, its right arm terminating in a huge, depleted-uranium-edged ax. There was nothing at all subtle about a *Hatchetman;* it was a brawler and a thug, a 'Mech for someone who liked close-in, dirty fighting.

The *Blade,* now, that roamed back and forth along the Northwind front—if any 'Mech could be described as elegant (besides, of course, her own beloved and specially modified *Ryoken II*), it was a *Blade*. Tall, fast-moving, and lightly armored, the *Blade* was a fencer's 'Mech, or a sprinter's.

Anastasia Kerensky was willing to bet that the delicate, yellow-haired Countess of Northwind piloted a *Blade*.

"Battlefield intelligence here," a voice said over the *Ryoken II*'s cockpit comms. "As of last report, Galaxy Commander, Paladin of the Sphere Ezekiel Crow uses a *Blade* BattleMech."

And I would have lost my bet, Anastasia thought. "So the *Hatchetman* belongs to the pretty little Countess."

"That is strongly probable."

"Who would have thought it?" Anastasia said. "Someday she and I will have to try one another—but not today, I think."

She looked out over the rainswept battlefield, and saw the tall, lean shape of the *Blade* coming toward her at a lope.

"Today I have a Paladin to kill."

Three 'Mechs against her one, and all the IndustrialMechs were sluggers—Tara Campbell brought her *Hatchetman* into action at a ground-shaking run, wondering as she did so whether the Wolves had modified the 'Mechs to be more suitable for battle.

As if in answer, the nearest of the three—a ForestryMech, by the huge chainsaw that formed its right arm—turned toward her and raised the other arm. An autocannon chittered, spouting bright flashes of light.

Whirlwind series autocannon, said her memory of intelligence reports and battles past. The *Hatchetman*'s armor could take it. A Whirlwind was a light weapon, suitable for impressing other Industrials. Let him see what a real BattleMech could do. She let her targeting computer handle the job of aiming, and fired the

Imperator Automatic Ultra 10 autocannon in the *Hatchetman*'s right torso.

The Imperator spat out hot flame and metal, forcing the modified ForestryMech to dodge, even as Tara sighted in on the one next nearest—a MiningMech, this time, probably with a bolt-on weapons package of its own. She targeted the MiningMech with her laser, vaporizing the pouring rain into a fog bank burned through with dazzling red light. The laser wouldn't do as much damage today as it could under better conditions—its beam was diffracted and dispersed and reflected by the sheets of falling rain—but the MechWarrior Tara was facing would still know that he'd been in a fight.

Sweat started beading on her forehead as the heat buildup in the *Hatchetman*'s cockpit ramped up. Firing two weapons at once, while attacking at a dead run—it was a damned good thing that her 'Mech had superior heat dissipation, and that she was fighting in an icy rainstorm on top of it.

Missiles flashed out ahead of her. She checked her cockpit displays, looking for the source. Not the ForestryMech—he was away to her left and going for position. The missiles came from the two remaining—they were both modified MiningMechs, all right, firing short-range missiles, in clusters, inbound.

Tara spun right to take the hits on the *Hatchetman*'s left torso. If she had to sacrifice a weapon, the autocannon would be the one to let go, because she was going to need the capabilities the hatchet gave her. The struggle with the three

'Mechs would be a knock-down hand-to-hand 'Mech fight, and a knock-down, hand-to-hand weapon was what she had—the great crushing ax at the end of her 'Mech's right arm.

49

Plains north of Tara
Northwind
June, 3133; local summer

Anastasia Kerensky turned her *Ryoken II* to face the onrushing *Blade*. The light 'Mech had nothing for armor, its lasers couldn't match her own heavier weapons, and she outweighed it by forty tons. This ought to be an easy kill, but she knew better than to make assumptions. A Paladin of the Sphere did not achieve that position by being an incompetent MechWarrior, and if Ezekiel Crow preferred to use a *Blade*, he must have learned years ago how to compensate for its disadvantages and make the most of its advantages.

The *Blade* was still coming at her, moving faster than before. The streaming rain blurred its outline in her view. Lightning flashed, dazzling her briefly—the fast-moving storm had to be almost directly above the battlefield by now, just as the Paladin's *Blade* was almost on top of her. She activated the *Ryoken II*'s jump jets and launched herself into the air.

The *Blade* raised its right arm, the Mydron Model RC Rotary autocannon tracking Anastasia as she leapt, the high-explosive, armor-piercing shells striking her legs and lower torso as she descended and brought her 'Mech's arms smashing down against the lighter *Blade*—and struck only air as the *Blade* spun away, using its greater speed and agility to twist and burn her with a medium-range laser all the way down.

She landed the *Ryoken II* unharmed on its feet, then buffeted the Paladin's *Blade* with one massive metal arm and laughed to see him fall, roll, and come back to his feet.

"That had to have hurt," she said, and powered up the twin lasers on the *Ryoken II*. "Now see how you like this."

The *Blade* turned and ran, heading back uphill toward the Highlander lines. The strokes of lightning that played across the sky illuminated its progress with a jerky, strobe-like light. The *Ryoken II*'s hammer blow and the *Blade*'s resulting fall had crippled the lighter 'Mech, and its normally graceful gait was clumsy and wavering.

Anastasia let out a whoop of savage delight, and gave chase.

Lightning flashed and zigzagged over the battlefield as Ezekiel Crow took his *Blade* up the long slope at a deliberately stumbling pace, with

Anastasia Kerensky's *Ryoken II* close at its heels. He gave ironic thanks to the deity he had not believed in since Chang-an burned that the Clans professed to be above deception and subterfuge.

They weren't, of course—in Crow's judgment, there was no man or woman living who was above deceit—but their disdain for the use of such tactics tended to make them exceptionally bad at recognizing deception in action. In her zeal to follow and finish off what she perceived as a damaged and failing 'Mech, Anastasia Kerensky gave no sign of realizing that his *Blade,* for all its tantalizing closeness and limping gait, nevertheless managed to stay ahead of her pursuing *Ryoken II* all the way up the hill.

Crow reached the crest line of the hill with a safe lead on the *Ryoken II,* and as soon as he was over the top and out of Anastasia's sight he put the *Blade* into a fast sprint. For what he was going to try next, he wanted to put plenty of downhill distance between himself and Kerensky.

Lightning flashed again overhead, multiple strokes coming close together, turning the *Ryoken II* into a stark picture in black and white as it strode inexorably into view on the crest line. Another blaze of lightning. Crow lifted his right arm and shot the *Blade*'s extended-range medium laser into the air over the *Ryoken II*'s shoulder. Lightning flashed again overhead—and the stroke followed the laser's trail of ionized air back down toward the nearest high target: Anastasia Kerensky's 'Mech.

Trails of electricity crawled over the *Ryoken II*'s armored surface like blue and purple worms. It took one step downhill, then another—slower and more awkward—before its systems seized up completely and it stiffened, toppled, and fell.

Tara Campbell felt the impact of the MiningMechs' short-range missiles as a series of explosions rippling up the *Hatchetman*'s left side, staggering her and driving her sideways. The Warrior in the ForestryMech saw his opportunity and charged, his 'Mech's huge chainsaw roaring.

That chainsaw could slice right through the *Hatchetman*'s light Durallex armor. He'd be going for her ax, Tara thought, and she didn't dare lose her primary weapon. The displays from her left side sensors were flickering, and the Imperator autocannon on that side was definitely jammed—all she had left there was the left arm itself. In a pinch it would make a good club, but nothing more than that.

She turned to face the onrushing ForestryMech, lit it up with her Defiance extended-range medium laser, then started the *Hatchetman* pacing into its charge in long, ground-eating strides, following the laser beam in. She was peripherally aware of the two MiningMechs to her right, both of them running toward her with the peculiar lumbering gait of Industrials.

Tara smiled grimly. The Warriors in the 'Mechs didn't know it, but they were at a disadvantage. Unless they'd trained in fighting together, in fighting as a team, she was free to treat everyone around her as an enemy, while the two of them had to worry about hitting her while at the same time not inflicting damage on each other by accident. Moreover, her plans and her actions would be instantaneous while they had to take time to communicate among themselves.

The ForestryMech was almost upon her, and she upon it. She jumped, cutting in her jets as she rose, and leaped over the top of the ForestryMech, kicking it in the head as she went over. The angular momentum of the combined jump-and-kick nearly tumbled her, but the *Hatchetman*'s gyros held her steady as she landed directly behind the ForestryMech.

Before the Steel Wolf MechWarrior could turn, Tara spun the more agile *Hatchetman* around, and the great metal ax lashed forward and down. The blade cut into the shoulder joint on the ForestryMech's right side, shearing through the layers and ropes of steel and myomer and rendering its chainsaw useless. The 'Mech still had its autocannon, but if she could stay behind it. . . .

She couldn't. The Miners were here now, rock cutters raised. Tara turned to her right, to the closest one, and lashed out with the hatchet. The MiningMech stepped back out of reach, then pressed forward again—the MechWarrior was going for Tara's hatchet arm with his rock cutter, and now it was Tara's turn to step back. The movement brought her no escape from danger—it took her instead into the range of the second MiningMech, which promptly seized the opportunity to start gnawing away with its rock cutter at the *Hatchetman*'s already damaged left side and arm.

Time to call for assistance. Three on one was all very well, but pride was for fools.

"Paladin Crow, get over here," Tara said into her 'Mech-to-'Mech comm link. "I've got some fresh carrion for you."

Meanwhile, she had to stay alive and keep fighting. The longer she kept this trio of 'Mechs engaged, the less damage they could do to other Highlander units who couldn't take the damage. She couldn't get her hatchet around to strike the nearest MiningMech—she had the other MiningMech coming up behind her, and the ForestryMech on her right side was turning to shoot at her with that little Whirlwind autocannon.

Little autocannon or not, at this distance the ForestryMech couldn't miss—not when its target was close enough to practice ballroom dancing with—and at such close range the Whirlwind's ammo would chew through the *Hatchetman*'s Durallex armor as if it wasn't even there.

Nothing for it, then, but to attack. She turned her 'Mech's laser against the MiningMech in front of her, switched the targeting on, and aimed for the head and the sensory bundles. She followed up the laser with an ax swing to the right, against the already damaged ForestryMech. This time she aimed low, for a leg, and struck her opponent in the hip. The blade of the hatchet crimped metal in what should have been moving parts—but which wouldn't be moving any longer.

She brought the hatchet back up to the ready position and jumped again, landing a short distance behind the ForestryMech. She pressed the *Hatchetman*'s left arm against the ForestryMech's torso and pushed.

With its crippled leg, the ForestryMech couldn't maintain its balance. It fell, tumbling to the ground beneath the legs of the MiningMech that Tara had just been fighting.

She struck out again with her hatchet, not caring now if the MiningMech's rock cutter came too close, and hooked the 'Mech's left arm. The MiningMech had only machine guns in that arm—no threat to a BattleMech. She pulled back on the hatchet arm in the same direction the MiningMech had already been going.

In her *Hatchetman*, she only outweighed the MiningMech by ten tons—little enough, so that she had to use wrestling tricks rather than raw strength to force the other to fall. But fall he did, with his legs entangled in the fallen ForestryMech. Tara leapt up, aided by her jump jets, and brought the *Hatchetman*'s forty-five-ton mass crashing down with both heels in the center of the MiningMech's back. MiningMech and ForestryMech were reduced to a tangle of crumpled metal that would take repair technicians weeks to sort out and fix.

The second MiningMech had not yet given up the fight, but was pressing in close. Four more short-range missiles fired from its torso. That's it, Tara said to herself. No more reloads until it gets back to a field armory. The MiningMech only had machine guns now. And she had speed on it.

She checked her heat dials. No, she *didn't*

have speed on it. If she didn't watch out, before very long she'd be sitting in a 'Mech that was overheated and refusing to move.

But the MiningMech didn't know that. Tara fired her laser full on into its midtorso.

Rainwater flashed into billowing clouds of steam around both of the 'Mechs as it fell onto their external heat sinks. Fog enshrouded them.

"Surrender," Tara said over the common 'Mech frequency that both the Highlanders and the Steel Wolves used. "You have no choice. You have no weapons."

"I have this," a voice came back. The MiningMech raised its rock cutter. "I will have you out of your tin can in a moment, my lady, and feed you to the dogs."

The speaker was a woman, from the sound of it—a light, high voice, made hoarse with tension. If we'd met under different circumstances, Tara thought, maybe I'd be buying her a beer instead of braining her.

Aloud she said, "You had your chance," stepped forward, and engaged the *Hatchetman*'s jets for another crushing leap.

The MiningMech broke and ran.

Tara came down, turned to give chase, and abruptly froze as the *Hatchetman*'s self-preservation clicked in, refusing to take any more heat-producing actions until some of the heat already released had a chance to dissipate.

It didn't matter, though; she wouldn't go unprotected while her 'Mech recovered. Infantry was coming up—scouts and engineers, wearing the uniforms of Northwind.

My people, Tara thought.

The engineers approached the two fallen Steel Wolf 'Mechs, and placed charges. Then one of the engineers attached demolition blocks around the MiningMech's entrance hatch.

Another soldier approached Tara. She turned on her outside microphones in time to hear the engineer saying, "Prefect, if you wish, could you call this stubborn bastard over your comms and tell him to come out with his hands up?"

"Yes," Tara replied on external circuit.

The trooper saluted.

She keyed the mike on the 'Mech common channel, and spoke.

"Steel Wolf, there is no dishonor in surrendering. Your 'Mech is immobilized, and my troops are wiring it for demolition even as we speak. It's up to you if you're inside when we blow it up."

A pause, and then the reply, "You would not."

"You had your chance," Tara said.

She addressed the engineers over her external speakers, but made sure that the intra-'Mech link was also open and live.

"I can't do a thing with him," Tara said to the engineers, over both circuits. "Destroy the 'Mech. It's no use to us, it's damaged already."

"No, wait!" came the voice of the Steel Wolf. "Will my friend in the ForestryMech and I be harmed if we surrender?"

"I guarantee that you will be treated with all honor," Tara said.

The rear hatch of the MiningMech opened. A young man emerged, his skimpy MechWarrior shorts and vest soaked with perspiration. The rain caught him and rendered him shivering.

"Take him to the rear. Take them both to the rear," Tara said. "Before they get hypothermia and die on us."

She checked her cockpit dials again. The heat was lower. The autoshutdown routine had worked and she could move again. The third 'Mech had gone . . . that way. She prepared to follow.

Before she could make a move, a Fox armored car bearing Northwind insignia approached. A short-range signal crackled over the *Hatchetman*'s inside speakers.

"Prefect—the Paladin needs you, now."

"I'm on my way," she replied.

She followed the Fox all the way back to the hill where Ezekiel Crow's *Blade* was standing and looking out over the field—a mass of rain-sodden ground, half-obscured by mist and drifting smoke, covered with crumpled machinery and the bodies of Wolves and Highlanders alike.

"My lady," he said over the command circuit as she approached. "Galaxy Commander Kerensky's 'Mech is disabled and the Wolves are running. I believe the day is ours."

50

White Horse Bar
City of Tara, Northwind
June, 3133; local summer

Drinks were on the house in the White Horse Bar—drinks were on the house in every bar in Tara, if you wore a Regimental uniform—and the tri-vid behind the counter was tuned to a news channel showing pictures of the Steel Wolves DropShips lifting from the salt flats beyond the Bloodstones. Will Elliot, who had found himself promoted to Corporal in the aftermath of the battles for Red Ledge Pass and the Plains of Tara, was happy to watch the tri-vid and nurse the same beer he'd purchased at the start of the evening. Jock Gordon and Lexa McIntosh, to either side of him at the counter, were both well on the way to becoming completely and happily drunk, and somebody was going to have to stay sober enough to see them back to barracks before morning.

Lexa raised her glass to the image of the departing DropShips. "Good riddance to bad rubbish, and don't come back!"

"We had them on the run," Jock said. "Once the aerospace fighters showed up from Halidon, we had them on the run. I still say that we shouldn't have let them go."

"The Countess didn't want to let them go," Lexa said. She emptied off her drink and gestured at the bartender for another of the same. "She wanted to chase them until they dropped and then cut them up into pieces. That's what everybody says."

"Everybody says a lot of things," said Will. He found it easy to believe that the Countess hadn't wanted to give up the pursuit—he and Lexa had gotten a good view from their foxhole of her three-on-one melee with the Steel Wolf IndustrialMechs, and the spectacle had left no doubt in his mind that Prefect Tara Campbell could be a brawler when she had to be, but he didn't think she was the type to become vengeful in victory.

Listen to yourself, he thought. Thinking you know what the Prefect thinks, just because you fought in the same battle as she did. You don't know anything about her worries, any more than she knows about yours.

He had to admit that he would have been feeling a good deal more vengeful himself toward Anastasia Kerensky and the Steel Wolves if things had turned out only a little worse. Liddisdale had been one of the mountain towns in the path of the enemy's advance, and the house Will grew up in had sheltered a Highlander missile battery for a few hours, until one of the Steel Wolves' MiningMechs had taken both house and defenders apart.

Will had heard the news from his mother. Jean Elliot had taken shelter with Old Angus and Robbie Macallan when the fighting started, and was staying in their mountain cabin until Will's sister in Kildare could make it across the mountains. He hadn't yet gone back to Liddisdale to look at the wreckage for himself, and wasn't sure that he wanted to.

The tri-vid news channel changed its picture from shots of departing DropShips to an image of the Fort, followed by a close-up of a dark-haired man in plain clothing. The identification block at the bottom of the tri-vid told the viewers that they were looking at a live image of Paladin Ezekiel Crow.

Will regarded the Paladin's projected features with mild curiosity. So this was a Paladin of the Sphere—not much to look at, considering that in popular stories all the Paladins were six feet tall and practically glowed with virtue. Ezekiel Crow was just another tired-looking survivor of the Wolves' invasion, as far as Will could tell.

"Is it true, my lord," said the voice of an off-camera news reporter, "that you told the Prefect to let the Steel Wolves go?"

Next to Will, Jock Gordon laughed. "Sounds like somebody else was wondering the same things we were."

"You think you're bright enough to wonder something new and different?" said Lexa. "Shut up and listen to the man."

"It's true that I advised the Prefect to that end," Crow was saying to the news reporter. "The Steel Wolves may have abandoned their allegiance to The Republic of the Sphere, but they are not yet such bitter enemies that Northwind may not need them some day as friends, and they know well enough who won this fight. Destroying them would only have given you an enemy who would hate you for generations. Better to let them go, with honor, in the hope of more peaceful days to come."

"How about the Prefect, my lord? Did she see things the same way, or is it true—as people are saying—that you used your authority to overrule her decision?"

Ezekiel Crow smiled. "I don't think the people of Northwind know their own Countess very well, if they're willing to believe that anybody—even a Paladin—could make Tara Campbell do something that she truly didn't want to do."

The news reporter's reply was lost to history, at least as far as Will Elliot was concerned, when Lexa McIntosh gave an approving and earsplitting whoop.

"That's our Countess!" Lexa shouted. "Here's to her!"

She drained her drink and sent the empty glass crashing to the floor. In the next breath, Jock Gordon followed her example, and within an instant the White Horse Bar was full of the noise of shouted toasts and breaking glass. Will hesitated only a moment longer, then threw down his own empty glass to mingle with the shards of all the others.

On the tri-vid, unheeded, the news channel went back to images of the Steel Wolf DropShips lifting, one by one.